Family Business III

Love And Honor

Family Business Series

JAN 17

CH

Family Business III
Love And Honor

Vanessa
Miller

Book 3
Family Business Series

Vanessa Miller
www.vanessamiller.com

Printed in the United States of America
© 2016 by Vanessa Miller

Praise Unlimited Enterprises
Charlotte, NC

Other Books by Vanessa Miller

Sunshine and Rain (rel. Oct. 29, 2016)
Family Business Book III (Love & Honor)
Family Business Book II (Sword of Division)
Family Business Book I
Rain in the Promised Land
After the Rain
How Sweet The Sound
Heirs of Rebellion
Heaven Sent
Feels Like Heaven
Heaven on Earth
The Best of All
Better for Us
Her Good Thing
Long Time Coming
A Promise of Forever Love
A Love for Tomorrow
Yesterday's Promise
Forgotten
Forgiven
Forsaken
Rain for Christmas (Novella)
Through the Storm
Rain Storm
Latter Rain

Abundant Rain

Former Rain

Anthologies (Editor)

Keeping the Faith

Have A Little Faith

This Far by Faith

EBOOKS

Love Isn't Enough

A Mighty Love

The Blessed One (Blessed and Highly Favored series)

The Wild One (Blessed and Highly Favored Series)

The Preacher's Choice (Blessed and Highly Favored Series)

The Politician's Wife (Blessed and Highly Favored Series)

The Playboy's Redemption (Blessed and Highly Favored Series)

Tears Fall at Night (Praise Him Anyhow Series)

Joy Comes in the Morning (Praise Him Anyhow Series)

A Forever Kind of Love (Praise Him Anyhow Series)

Ramsey's Praise (Praise Him Anyhow Series)

Escape to Love (Praise Him Anyhow Series)

Praise For Christmas (Praise Him Anyhow Series)

His Love Walk (Praise Him Anyhow Series)

Could This Be Love (Praise Him Anyhow Series)

Song of Praise (Praise Him Anyhow Series)

Prologue

When Demetrius Shepherd told Angel that their home had gone up in flames and that she and the kids couldn't come home, but instead needed to drive all the way to her parents' house in North Carolina, she felt as if her life had gone up in flames right along with that house. Her husband was sending her away at a time in their marriage when they needed to be together.

They'd had ten blissful years of marriage, but so much had gone wrong in this last year that the ten previous years no longer seemed to matter. Needless to say, Angel was frantic with worry over the state of her marriage as she drove her children to Winston-Salem. But the farther she drove away from Ohio, her burning home and all the problems with Demetrius, she could see God's hand at work. First off, for Demetrius to be sending them away like this, she knew that the house didn't just catch on fire, but someone had burned it down... someone who was probably, once again, trying to get at Don Shepherd, Demetrius' drug dealing father.

Angel would walk through the fire for Demetrius, but the Shepherd family business had caused her more heartache than she cared to think about. There were too many other things she needed to concern herself with right now.

Angel touched her stomach, and as she did so, love and joy bubbled in her spirit. She was going to have another child. A child that Demetrius didn't want because they didn't know if this baby was his or Frankie Day's... Mama's baby, Daddy's maybe was what they were dealing with. Her husband had wanted her to abort the baby, so that they could get on with their lives and put a period on the horrible things that happened to her. But how could she kill an innocent baby because of the actions of an evil man who was now dead and gone?

Yes, Frankie had raped her, so it was a toss-up as to who this child's father was. Angel didn't think it mattered, because Demetrius' father, Don, had murdered Frankie and Angel hadn't shed one tear for the man. Now all she wanted to do was give birth to her child and pray that this child was hers and Demetrius'. The only trouble was, Angel didn't know how to tell Demetrius that she had decided not to have the abortion he had demanded of her.

And anyway, Angel didn't see the harm in having the baby no matter who the biological father was; because Frankie Day was her oldest son's biological father. Yes, she had previously been in a so-called relationship with that monster.

She met Frankie after running away from home at the age of sixteen. For a time, Angel convinced herself that she was in love with him. But once DeMarcus was born, Frankie showed his true colors. That's when she met Demetrius. Even though Demetrius grew up in a crime family, he had always been gentle with her.

Demetrius knew that his father had sent her to Frankie's house. He knew that Frankie had trapped her in that house and took what only belonged to her husband. Demetrius had been so loving after the incident with Frankie. It was only after he'd discovered that she was pregnant, that he turned on her. How could he expect her to get rid of a child that could just as well be their love child... and even if this baby did belong to Frankie, Demetrius had already adopted DeMarcus and loved him like he was his own biological father.

Angel was so full of trepidation during the drive to North Carolina, but the moment she pulled into her parents' driveway, it was as if her whole world had changed. The kids jumped out of the car and ran toward the porch. Angel lowered her head and silently prayed that God would work things out for her family. But even as she prayed, Angel knew that she and Demetrius would never be the same, not just because of the baby, but also because of what else she had done today.

Maxine opened the door and hugged each of her grandsons, and then made her way to Angel's car. Angel rolled down the window and held up her cell phone. "I need to call Demetrius and then I'll be right in."

"I'll make us some tea and then you can tell me, once and for all, what is going on that keeps sending you and the kids back here without your husband."

"I will Mama, I'll tell you the truth this time." She wasn't about that life anymore… no more lies, she was going to tell her parents everything and then ask them to pray with her, like they used to do when she was a little girl. Ever since Angel reunited with her parents, she had been lying to them. She had asked Demetrius to tell her parents that he was DeMarcus' biological father and that they were engaged to be married. At the time, she and Demetrius weren't engaged, but he'd understood that since Angel's parents were not just church going people, but pastors, she didn't want to tell them everything that had gone down after she ran away, so he'd gone along with it.

Her lies had started to unravel during Angel's last visit to her parents'. DeMarcus had overheard Angel and Demetrius arguing about Frankie Day, and he'd heard Angel admit that Frankie was his father. DeMarcus told her father, and consequently, Angel had been forced to admit the truth.

But Angel was tired of lying and concealing the truth. She had decided never to lie when the truth was readily available ever again. Not even to save her marriage. She took a deep breath as she called Demetrius. He picked up after the first ring.

"I was just getting ready to call. Did you make it to your parents' yet?"

"I'm here. The kids are in the house with my mom, but I wanted to talk to you before I went in. I think we need to clear the air about some things."

"I know you're worried. But I'm just thankful that you and the kids weren't in the house when it went up in flames." Demetrius cleared his throat as he continued, "We can replace clothes and furniture."

"Was it deliberate?"

"Naw, I think one of us must have left something on and since no one was home, what could have been a small fire, just kept on blazing until it burnt the whole house down."

"Are you sure, Demetrius?"

"Well, as sure as I can be. The fire marshal will do the investigation, and we'll know more after that."

"Okay, well, to tell you the truth, right now the house is the least of my worries. I called to tell you that I didn't have the abortion. I'm going to keep our baby."

"You don't know for sure it's *Our* baby," Demetrius told her as his voice hardened.

"And you don't know for sure that it's not our baby."

"Whatever."

"No, it's not whatever, Demetrius. This is our baby. And he or she deserves to live just as much as our other kids. But there's something else you need to know."

"As far as I'm concerned, we're not done with the first thing you sprang on me, so we can't just jump to another subject."

But Angel was done discussing the child that was growing inside of her. She was having this baby and that was it, end of discussion. In truth, she wondered if what she had to say next would make Demetrius angrier than he was at this moment. No matter what happened from this point forward, Angel needed Demetrius to know about the joy she found at an abortion clinic of all places. "When you sent me to that place today, God had a woman waiting for me. I don't know if she was an angel or simply a minister of the gospel. Her name is Patricia and she told me that God had something special in mind for our son. So, don't you see, Demetrius? I couldn't kill this child, because I am supposed to give birth to him and then give him back to God."

Angel could hear breathing on the other end of the phone, but Demetrius hadn't uttered a word. "You don't believe me, do you?"

"Right now I don't know what to believe… look, I've got a lot of things to take care of around here. So, I'll call you back later." Demetrius hung up the phone.

But Angel wasn't finished. She wanted to tell Demetrius about the way God set her free today. After meeting her parents, Demetrius feared that Angel would one day become a 'Jesus freak', as he called it. Angel had assured him that she wouldn't and that they would live happily ever after in his world. But that was no longer true. Angel couldn't stay in Demetrius' world anymore, not without God. Her husband would just have to understand that this day was special to her. She wouldn't remember it as the day her house burned down, and she had to flee the city... No. Angel would remember this glorious day, as the day she gave her heart back to God, and willingly became a 'Jesus freak'.

One

As far as Demetrius Shepherd was concerned, his wife had lost her whole mind. If she thought he would ever take care of a child belonging to Frankie Day, she had another thought coming. He was going to get rid of that baby one way or the other. He was angry at the news his wife had given him, but he couldn't spend the rest of the day dwelling on it. Right now he had much more pressing issues to deal with... like the Columbians.

Demetrius' dad had been the kingpin and everybody in Ohio knew it. Don Shepherd handled his business with an iron fist and made just as many enemies as friends. Don had even made an enemy out of his own son, which was the reason Don was now sitting in jail, waiting to go to a trial in which Demetrius would be the primary witness against him. His father had killed people for less.

But Don had sent Angel to Frankie, so he was responsible for everything Demetrius was now suffering. Demetrius had become so enraged after Frankie violated his wife, that he told the police everything they needed to know to make charges stick against the man who'd been like Teflon to them for so many years. But Demetrius didn't know that his father's drug empire had grown so large because he was being backed by the Columbians. And these dudes didn't play.

Two men from the organization had visited him after Don had been arrested. They told him that he would have to take over for his father, but Demetrius had never wanted any parts of the type of crime his father committed on the daily. So, he'd said that he wouldn't be able to help them. The men calmly walked out of his office and the next thing Demetrius knew, his house was on fire.

Demetrius was now at the jail house waiting to talk with his father, because he needed to know what to do. When Don sat down behind the glass and picked up the phone to begin their conversation, Demetrius leaned forward as he asked, "How you holding up?"

"You know how I do. I'm gon' be alright."

Don Shepherd had always seemed like a god to Demetrius. His father was the man, no ifs, ands or buts about it, and Demetrius had practically worshipped him. Don said no more baseball, and Demetrius complied. Don said you're joining the family business, and Demetrius fell in line. In all his thirty-seven years, Demetrius had only defied his father a handful of times. But he had never turned on his father as he'd done a month ago. Demetrius had become so enraged that he hadn't been thinking straight... didn't realize that he would one day need his father again.

Demetrius also didn't realize that his father was just as enraged by what happened to Angel as he was. Demetrius had gone to Frankie Day's house to kill him for what he'd done to Angel. But that's when he found the man strung up in his basement with a knife stuck in his chest. Right away, Demetrius knew that his father had taken care of business so Demetrius wouldn't have a murder on his sheet. And it was at that moment that he wished he hadn't turned rat. There was nothing he could do about it though, because Don had been picked up by the cops that very morning. "I'm sorry, Dad."

Don shook his head. "I know why you did it. I'm not sweating it."

"My house caught on fire."

"I heard," Don said, then added, "Got to make sure that doesn't happen again."

"How?"

"You're in charge now. Do you hear me, Demetrius? You the man. So, you got to handle things until I figure a way out of here."

How was he going to handle things? Demetrius was no Don Shepherd. He'd beat down more men than he could count, but he'd never killed anyone and he detested the selling of drugs in the community. Crackheads were tearing down everything, robbing everybody, just so they could get that next fix. "I'm not you, Dad. This isn't the life I want for myself, nor the business I want my kids in."

Don smirked, puffed out his chest. "You didn't have a problem with this little family business of ours while it was putting food on your table, and keeping a real nice roof over my grandkids' heads."

"That's not going to help my kids when I'm locked up in here with you, now is it?" Demetrius knew that he'd earned a good living by turning a blind eye to how Don earned his money, but what he was now being asked to do was way more than he could handle.

Don turned his head and eyed the guard, the guard nodded and then moved about three feet away. Don then turned back to his son, put the phone close to his mouth and said, "I'm not trying to end up with a shank in my back just because you don't want to man-up and do what's got to be done for this family. And just in case you think all your problems will go away once I'm dead... think again. Because they ain't gon' stop with me. You, Angel and them grandbabies will all be a memory. Now do you want that, boy?"

Some nights when Demetrius closed his eyes and fell asleep, he'd find himself as a member of a non-violent, non-criminal, regular breadwinning kind of family. He and his wife talked about things like saving for college for the kids, and argued about being late for church on Sunday. But when he woke up, he was forced to accept the fact that his dreams were sweet, but life was a nightmare. "What am I supposed to do now? Sell the strip mall I just worked so hard putting together?"

"No, we're going to need that strip mall. But you'll want to hire a few more people to help you manage it, because you're going to be focused on getting our real business back up and running."

"I see the truth now Dad, my strip mall is just a dream. The family business is my reality."

Don's eyebrow lifted. "Boy, what are you mumbling about?"

"Nothing, Dad. I get it. I know what I'm supposed to do… Just don't know how to do it since I've never been involved in that side of the business."

"Don't worry about that. Al is going to meet up with you this week. He'll get you going."

Demetrius' eyes bugged out. "Al hates me!"

"Al is like an uncle to you. He don't hate you… just wishes that you'd get it together. And hear me good, Demetrius, this is your last chance to make things right."

"Oh, so now you're threatening me too?"

Don shook his head. "You're in the big leagues now boy. I'm your daddy, so even though I would have killed another man for some of the things you got away with… the Columbians don't have no blood connection with you." Don hung up the phone and stood up.

The guard came over, Demetrius heard him say, "I'm sorry, Don, but I've got to do this," then put the handcuffs back on his father and patted him on the shoulder as he escorted Don out of the visitation room.

Don might be locked up, but he was still the kingpin; even behind bars the man wasn't bowing down to nobody, they were all bowing down to him. Demetrius, on the other hand, left the jail house feeling as if he had just been shackled and put in chains himself. His life was never going to be the same. What could he do, but go with it. Because if he didn't and his family was murdered, Demetrius couldn't even fathom how he would get over that kind of nightmare.

He got in his car and drove over to an empty field on the outskirts of town. He walked the land, getting a feel for the expansiveness of it. Demetrius liked the fact that there was no sign of life for miles around. No homes were being built over here; no gas stations or convenience stores. Nothing but the crickets and the land.

His family would be safe here, Demetrius was sure of it. He was going to meet with the real estate agent first thing in the morning to sign the contract. Then Demetrius was going to build a fortress to protect his family.

"Well, well, would you look at Judas," Al Gamer said as he stepped onto the land that Demetrius had been surveying.

Demetrius swung around to face Al, his dad's enforcer. "Following me?"

"Yep." he said, unapologetically.

Demetrius looked passed Al, pointing out toward the street. "One day real soon you're not even going to be able to get on this street without going through the security gate."

Al laughed at him. He then patted Demetrius on the back as he said, "A security system hasn't been made that I can't get through… them Columbians ain't gone stop at your so-called security gate either. So, I suggest that you do as you're told."

Two

Angel only expected to be in Winston-Salem for a couple of months during the summer, but as time passed and Demetrius hadn't finished building their new home, Angel had no choice but to enroll the kids in school. DeMarcus was a football genius, he was bound for a college scholarship and the NFL, and everybody knew it. Scouts had come to the summer league her father had put him in to watch him play; and every high school coach in Winston-Salem had practically offered her a home in their district, if DeMarcus would play for them.

Angel wasn't about to move her children into another home, when she didn't know how soon they would be returning to Dayton. She informed each mouth-watering coach that the Shepherds were only part-time residents of Winston-Salem, so DeMarcus would be attending the school in her parents' district.

She and Demetrius talked every evening. He'd told her which coaches to watch out for, the ones who seemed like they wanted to put the weight of the team on DeMarcus' shoulders. It had happened to Demetrius when he was in high school. He'd been a baseball star destined for the Major Leagues. But he'd slid wrong and broke his ankle.

"We've got to be smart about this, Angel." Demetrius told her. "I dealt with too many coaches that were in it for themselves, and how good I could make their team look. I doubt if they stopped to think about my future. It was just a foregone conclusion that I would make it to the Majors. But that never happened for me."

Angel knew that thinking about baseball and the what-could-have-beens always put Demetrius in a dark place. "How is the house coming along?"

"The builders are working as fast as they can, but it's going to take about five more months before it's finished."

But the baby will be born by then, was what Angel wanted to say, but instead she told him, "Dee hates his new school. All he ever talks about is going home. I don't think Winston-Salem will ever win his heart." Dee was short for Demetrius Junior. And he was an eleven-year old replica of his father.

"That's my boy. I bet Dontae isn't thinking about coming home. That boy is probably out in the back yard chasing down as many bugs as he can find."

Dontae was seven, going on eight and he did indeed spend a great deal of time chasing and collecting bugs, toads and lizards. "What can I say, his mother is from the country. So, it's good to know that one of our sons enjoys nature." But that was as far as their conversation would go concerning their children. Demetrius never asked about the child that was growing inside of her.

There was so much that Angel wanted to share with Demetrius about this baby, because she could feel him growing. Not only that, when she was five months along, the baby leaped in her womb with such force that she almost fell backward. She remembered the exact moment that it happened. Her father was standing behind the pulpit on Sunday morning preaching his heart out. Pastor Marvin Barnes was reading out of Isaiah chapter 40. These were the words Angel heard as her baby started jumping around as if he wanted to be turned loose on the world:

"Comfort, yes, comfort My people!" Says your God. "Speak comfort to Jerusalem, and cry out to her, that her warfare is ended, that her iniquity is pardoned; For she has received from the Lord's hand double for all her sins." The voice of one crying in the wilderness: "Prepare the way of the Lord; make straight in the desert a highway for our God. Every valley shall be exalted and every mountain and hill brought low; the crooked places shall be made straight and the rough places smooth; The glory of the Lord shall be revealed, and all flesh shall see it together; for the mouth of the Lord has spoken."

Angel had carried three other children for nine full months and none of them had ever done summersaults in her belly; or kicked like they were trying to get out as if entering this cruel world was something he was destined to do. Putting a hand on her belly, Angel thought back to the day she discovered that the child she carried was special. It was also the same day that she had planned to kill her baby…

Angel was tired of arguing with Demetrius so she gave in to his demands and drove over to the abortion clinic. But as she pulled into the parking lot the first thing she saw was people holding picket signs.

One sign said, 'Don't Kill Your Baby... Every Life Matters. Then another sign had on it, 'Jeremiah 1:5'.

The scripture was not written on that poster, but it didn't have to be. It was the same scripture her father used to read to her when she was a child: Before I formed you in the womb I knew you; Before you were born I sanctified you.

Tears were blurring her eyes as the woman who'd been holding the 'Every Life Matters' poster knocked on her door. Angel wiped her face and rolled down the window.

The woman asked, "Would you like to talk to someone?"

Angel nodded as she unlocked the door and allowed the woman to get in the car.

The woman extended her hand. "I'm Patricia Miller-Harding. You don't have to cry anymore because God sent me here for you."

"Why would God send you to me?"

"You don't believe me?" Patricia put a gentle hand on Angel's shoulder as she said, "I know everything about you, Angel."

"How do you know my name?"

"God has given me a glimpse into your life... I know that your upbringing was all about the Lord and growing closer to Him. Until your parent's divorce, you had even planned to go into the ministry yourself. But then you ran away, moved in with a street-wise guy, and when he tossed you out, instead of humbling yourself and going back to your parents, who had re-married, you started stripping and then you fell in love with another criminal. You married him and now he has you here, about to kill one of God's soldiers."

"Who are you?" were the only words Angel could form. She was stunned that this woman could so read her. What was going on?

"I'm a friend, sent by the Lord with a message for you."

"What's the message," Angel asked, still feeling a little devastated by the way she'd just been read.

Patricia looked directly into Angel's eyes and held onto her hands as she said, "Thus says the Lord, 'you were born to serve God, you chose not to... but this baby you are carrying will not be swayed by the enemy. He will do great and mighty things for the Lord'."

Angel didn't know what to make of that woman's comments that day, but she believed she had heard from God. That was the same day that Angel gave her heart back to God. When she was a child, Angel wanted nothing more than to follow in her father's footsteps and become a preacher.

But then her father cheated on her mother and they were subsequently divorced. Her father's actions brought on a downward spiral in Angel's life that caused her to turn away from God. Her mother and father had remarried after being divorced for a few years, her father had been forgiven by God and his wife for his foolish behavior. But it still took Angel fifteen years to find her way back to God.

At that moment, Angel decided that she would do nothing to hinder the relationship with God, the child in her womb must develop in order to become this vessel that will be used to further the Kingdom.

She sat down at the kitchen table and opened her bible to the book of Isaiah and began reading in the same chapter her father had read out of during service that morning. But this time Angel started at verse 6:

The voice said, "Cry out!" And he said, "What shall I cry?" All flesh is grass, and all its loveliness is like the flower of the field... O Zion, you who bring good tidings, get up into the high mountain; O Jerusalem, You who bring good tidings, lift up your voice with strength, lift it up, be not afraid; say to the cities of Judah, "Behold your God!" Behold the Lord God shall come with a strong hand, and His arm shall rule for Him; behold, His reward is with Him.

Angel suddenly put the bible down and gasped for air. It felt as if her soul was being ripped out of her body as the baby seemed to attack her with his desire to get out. She screamed.

Maxine ran into the kitchen. "What's wrong? It's not the baby is it?"

"He's kicking my guts out." Angel then took a few deep breaths, trying to calm herself down. He head slumped back against the chair. "It stopped."

"Come on, let me take you to the hospital. If he's kicking that bad, then something must be wrong." Maxine grabbed her keys and tried to help Angel out of her seat.

Angel shook her head. "He's calm now. It was the bible passage I was reading that got him all excited. I have to watch what I read to this boy, because he is anxious to get out into the world and begin his mission."

"What mission?" the look in Maxine's eyes indicated that she was clueless.

"Sit down for a minute, Mama. I think it's finally time that I tell you everything that's going on."

"You mean there is even more to this story than what you've already told me." Maxine pulled out a chair. "If that's the case, then you're right. I need to sit down."

Angel reached a hand out to her mother as she sat down. "I'm not trying to keep secrets from you anymore. I'd rather tell you about my faults and sins, and then ask you to help me pray about it."

"Amen to that girl, because we both know that God answers prayers."

"He does," Angel agreed. "He saved my soul and I am so grateful for the years that you spent praying for me. But I have to tell you what brought me to the Lord that day."

Maxine shook her head. "That's between you and God, baby. You don't owe me or your daddy anything. We're just happy that the good Lord brought you back to us."

The two women hugged but then Angel told her, "I appreciate that, Mom. But I need to tell you about my journey because it involves my baby. You see, even though Demetrius loved me and stood by me after what Frankie did...." Angel couldn't bring herself to say the words, but had somehow managed to get the sordid story out enough for her parents to understand when they first arrived at their doorstep. "But when he found out I was pregnant, he changed on me. He wanted me to abort the baby."

Shame shadowed Angel's face as she continued. "I kept saying no, that this baby was a life just like any other. But Demetrius became so hateful that I thought I had no other choice." Tears streamed down Angel's face as she admitted. "I made an appointment to kill my baby. But when I showed up, I met this woman named Patricia. I truly believe she was sent from God. She told me that even though I walked away from the ministry that God had for me, the baby I am carrying would do great things for God.

"I was so distraught over the fact that I had entertained the idea of killing this baby, that I drove over to KeKe's house and prayed the prayer of salvation with her."

Maxine got out of her chair and started shouting in her kitchen, between the island and the stove.

Angel smiled at her mom's antics. "You haven't even heard the good part yet, and you're already shouting."

"If my baby, deciding not to kill her baby and then her coming home to the Lord all in the same morning isn't something to shout about, then I don't know what is."

23

"Okay, I'll give you that. But after giving my life to God, I stayed away from the house for hours because I had just done two things to royally tick Demetrius off." She side eyed her mom, checking her expression as she explained. "Demetrius isn't a bad guy, he just doesn't understand spiritual things… and I know you warned me about marrying someone who doesn't share my belief system. But at the time, Demetrius and I only believed in each other."

Maxine sat back down next to her daughter and patted her hand, letting her know that she wasn't there to judge, only support.

"I was glad that I decided to keep my baby and I was thankful that I now had God in my life again, but I was terrified that Demetrius just might leave me for both decisions. So, I spent a few hours driving around, praying, and I even picked up a bible… Later, I picked the kids up from activities and was heading home when, Demetrius called and told me that the house was on fire, and that I needed to come directly here rather than stay there with him. I knew that God had just answered my prayers, because if I would have stayed, who knows if Demetrius would have convinced me to go through with the abortion? And if I had gone through with the abortion, I never would have received the confirmation that my son is going to be something special in the body of Christ."

The look in Maxine's eyes said it all. She was fascinated by Angel's story. "I remember when your dad and I first discovered that you would one day minister to the people of God. You were in the backyard standing behind some makeshift podium, preaching your little heart out to your four-member congregation."

"Well my baby isn't even out of the womb and he's already giving me signs. When daddy read out of Isaiah chapter 40, my baby started fighting to get out, and then again just now as I tried to read the rest of that chapter.

"Mama, I think this baby is going to be some kind of modern day John the Baptist. And I don't know whether to be excited or terrified about that."

Three

Demetrius was in his business office meeting with each of the owners and/or general managers of each of the stores and restaurants in his strip mall. He gave each of them the same spiel. It went like, "A package will be delivered to your store each month. I will pay you two thousand each month for receiving it. But I cannot emphasize enough that the package must never be opened. All you will have to do is hand it off to the person who comes around to pick it up each month. Got me?"

There were now twenty stores in the strip mall, four of them were directly owned by Demetrius, so he hired general managers to manage the place as if they themselves owned it. But since he was the actual owner, Demetrius offered the general managers half of the amount he was giving the owners for receiving those packages for him each month. His day was going smoothly. He was getting everything set up for this drug empire that he would now have to run. Demetrius only had one problem… well two, but he was still deciding if the last problem was really a problem.

The first issue occurred when he called KeKe James into his office. She had recently taken over as general manager of the soul food restaurant and was doing her thang. Community support for the restaurant had increased by 30% since KeKe took over. But that didn't mean Demetrius was into all of this 'Praise the Lord' and 'won't He do it' stuff she was always saying as she talked with the customers.

And now, Ms.-Holy-Roller had the audacity to sit in his face and deny his request. "I know you didn't just say no to me. I own that restaurant in case you forgot."

KeKe took a deep breath, steepled her hands as she responded to her employer. "I respect the fact that you own the restaurant and I appreciate every opportunity you and Angel have given to me."

KeKe used to be strung out on crack. But once Children Services took her children, something snapped… it woke her up. She decided she couldn't live like that anymore and came to Demetrius' drive-thru and begged him for a job. He had been about to say no, but Angel stopped him, said she saw something in KeKe and thought the girl just needed a break. Well he'd given KeKe that break, and now she was acting very ungrateful, and Demetrius didn't like it one bit.

"And I'm not trying to tell you how to run your business," KeKe continued. "I'm just saying that I cannot hold packages for you, especially since I think the package might be something illegal."

Demetrius exploded out of his seat. "Do you know who I am?"

A touch of fear came over KeKe, even so, she said, "Demetrius, I love you like a brother. You've done more for me than anyone in my own family would have ever done. But I am a servant of God first and I must follow His lead, before I follow yours. You also know that I lost my children once because of the way I lived my life. Now that they have been given back to me, I promised the Lord that I would never do anything to have them taken away again."

He wanted to fire her. How dare she accuse him of trying to get her kids taken away? If it wasn't for him giving her a job and helping her get that apartment, she would have never got those kids back. The words, 'you're fired' were on the tip of his tongue, but

Demetrius knew he'd have all kinds of problems with Angel if he fired her friend. He didn't need that drama and he didn't need Angel knowing what he was up to.

"Get out of my office, KeKe."

KeKe didn't have to be told twice, she jumped up and jetted for the door.

Demetrius stopped her as she opened the door. "This conversation doesn't make it back to Angel, do you understand me?"

"I wouldn't bust you out like that Demetrius. I know you're in a no-win situation right now. But I'm praying that God would free you from your father's legacy."

As KeKe left his office, Demetrius didn't know whether to thank her for praying or to inform her that he didn't need her prayers. But before he could make up his mind, problem number two strutted into his office. She was holding a box of donuts from the donut shop that she and her father owned. It was one of the first businesses seen as people drove through the plaza. Business was good for them, so Jasmine Turner often brought him donuts as a thank you for giving them such a good location.

Trouble was, she also teased him with those bedroom eyes of hers. But it wasn't just Jasmine's eyes that caught Demetrius' attention, the girl had hips and curves that made him sea sick, just watching as she walked in and out of his office.

"That doesn't look like the container your donuts come in," he said as Jasmine handed over the food she'd carried into his office.

"A man can't live on donuts alone. Since your wife still hasn't come back home, I thought you could use a home cooked meal."

Demetrius shook his head and tried to give the Styrofoam container back to Jasmine. "I can't take food from your family. I can ride over to Burger King or Long John Silver's for lunch."

"I wouldn't hear of it. And besides, it's not like I have kids or anything. I cooked that food for my dad, and I brought you the left overs."

The smells coming out of that container were like down home cooking. The kind of cooking he could get at his soul food restaurant any day of the week. But Demetrius didn't like going in there all that much, because he'd have to listen to KeKe blessing the Lord and praising His Holy name. It was just too much for him to deal with and if things weren't so rocky between him and Angel, Demetrius would have fired the girl, and then gone into his restaurant to eat dinner.

He opened the container and his eyes feasted on fried chicken, macaroni and cheese, greens, yams and cornbread. "You get down like this?"

"You better know it," Jasmine said as she rubbed against him. "I get down in other ways too. You need to come see about me." Jasmine then turned and swiveled those hips of hers out the door.

Demetrius rushed to the glass door and watched as Jasmine made her way to the donut shop. When she was halfway there, she turned and waved at him. Demetrius jumped back. He'd been caught looking thirsty.

He sat back down behind his desk, trying to get his mind back on the day's work, but his eyes kept drifting to that container. Angel could burn in the kitchen. That was one of the reasons Demetrius married her, besides the fact that he loved her more than anything else this world had to offer. But Angel betrayed him when she decided to have that baby rather than get rid of it and let them get on with their lives.

Demetrius wanted to call his wife, he wanted to know how she was doing, but he didn't want to hear not one word about that baby.

So, he didn't make the call he desperately wanted to make, but instead he leaned back in his chair and started eating the food Jasmine brought him. After about the third bite, he realized that even though Jasmine's dinner wasn't quite as tasty as Angel's, it was still good... good enough.

~~~~

"Mama, come quick. I need help!" Angel screamed at the top of her lungs and kept on screaming until her bedroom door swung open.

Marvin and Maxine rushed in the room, they were panting and sweating. "What's happened? What's wrong?" Marvin asked as he was the first to regain his breath after he and his wife ran up the stairs.

"I think my water broke."

"But you're only seven months along," Maxine said as if that simple fact would make the baby wait.

Marvin pulled back the covers to see if the bed was wet. "Oh my sweet baby Jesus. Call the ambulance, Maxine."

Maxine glanced around her husband's shoulder and started screaming.

"What's wrong, Mama?"

Pointing at the bed, Maxine screamed "You're bleeding!"

"I'm what?" Angel attempted to sit up, but she felt so weak, that her head fell back onto the pillow.

Marvin shouted at Maxine again. "Go call an ambulance!"

She rushed out of the room, he sat down next to Angel and held onto her hand. "Are you hurting anywhere, honey?"

She shook her head. "I had been reading the bible, then the baby started moving around, like he just couldn't get comfortable. So, started singing to him, thinking that would calm him down. But then

I felt this pain like he was ripping my body apart… I think I passed out and when I woke up the bed felt wet, so I thought my water broke."

Her father picked up the bible that was lying next to her and glanced at the chapter she had been reading. The bible was turned to Matthew Chapter 3 which read:

In those days John the Baptist came preaching in the wilderness of Judea, and saying, "Repent, for the kingdom of heaven is at hand!" For this is he who was spoken of by the prophet Isaiah, saying: "The voice of one crying in the wilderness: 'prepare the way of the Lord; Make His paths straight.'"

When Pastor Marvin Barnes read those words he fell on his knees, grabbed hold of Angel's hand again and then he placed his other hand on her belly as he went before the Lord in prayer. "Oh my God, my good Lord in heaven. You have not forgotten this family, even though we have strayed away from You at times, and I thank You for that. Father, You know that neither I nor Angel were able to walk upright before You as we fell prey to the wickedness this world has to offer. But there is one coming, this babe that You have anointed as a modern day John-the-Baptist…

"I pray that You make his way straight. Do not allow this child to be ensnared by the trapping of this world, but let him accomplish everything You have him on earth to do."

"Daddy, I don't feel so good." Angel's pupils dilated and the skin around and her face and neck was changing.

"Help us, Lord. Keep Angel and this baby alive so the mission You have set forth can be accomplished. Don't let the enemy steal them away like this." Pastor Marvin Barnes moved out of the way, but kept right on praying even after the paramedics came into the room and placed Angel on the stretcher. Pastor Barnes was working too… He was busy calling on the Lord.

"Mama… Mama, what's wrong?" DeMarcus said as the kids watched the paramedics bring their mother down the stairs.

"She's going to the hospital, but she'll be alright," Maxine told the kids.

"I'm going too, Demetrius Jr. informed them.

Angel was barely conscious. Marvin knew that she wouldn't want the boys to see her like this. So, he told them, "Your grandmother will ride in the ambulance with your mother. And I'll ride you boys over to the hospital later this afternoon."

"I'm calling my daddy," DeMarcus said as his mother was being lifted into the ambulance.

"That's a good idea, Grandson. Go call your daddy. He should be here with his wife," Marvin told him.

Four

"Why don't you ever take me over to the house you're building? Why do we always have to meet up at a hotel?" Jasmine asked as she and Demetrius lay in bed together.

"Where else are we supposed to go? You still live at home with your daddy, and I doubt that he'd want me laying up with you at his house."

She shoved him. "I'm not talking about my house and you know it."

"Then I don't know where else you want to meet up." Demetrius turned towards her and lifted himself up as he leaned on one elbow. He waited, thinking this was Jasmine's way of asking him to set her up in an apartment. Jasmine was twenty four so it was time for her to be out on her own. And he might just be willing to help her get a place.

But Jasmine had something else in mind. "Why don't you ever take me to the house you're building? From what I hear, it's basically done."

Demetrius flopped back on his pillow and grimaced. "You can't go to my house, Jasmine. And I thought you understood that."

"What am I supposed to understand?"

Demetrius had been out of the dating game for so long that he'd completely forgotten how clingy these chicks could get. But this one wasn't just clingy, she clearly didn't know her place. "I'm not taking you to the house I'm building for my wife and kids; that will never happen."

"Why not?" Jasmine's eyes became glassy. "We been together three, four nights a week for the past month. You haven't even thought about bringing your wife home, so you must not want her."

Getting out of the bed and throwing on his jeans, Demetrius told her, "Don't question me about my wife. It's none of your business."

"It certainly is my business. You and I are together… your so-called wife hasn't been here in months. So, I have a right to ask about us. What you gon' do Demetrius? You gon' be with me or what?"

He stared her as he leaned against the dresser, getting ready to break down the real, real, but his cell phone rang. He saw that it was the landline at Angel's parent's house and ignored it. Then he received a 911 text and the cell rang again. Demetrius answered that time.

"Daddy, you have to get down here quick."

It was DeMarcus and he was crying. "What's wrong son? Why are you crying?"

"It's Mama. She's been rushed to the hospital. There was blood all over her bed and I don't even know if she was breathing when she left the house."

"What!" Demetrius shouted. "Who's at the house with you?"

"Papa is here. He's taking us to the hospital this afternoon."

"Put him on the phone."

The line went silent for a moment then Pastor Barnes said, "We're sure sorry to call you like this Demetrius. Wish we had better news."

"What are you talking about?" Demetrius was frantic. His hand went to his head as his heart just about broke inside his chest. There was no way that this man was about to tell him that his wife was dead. He wasn't a praying man, and certainly didn't feel worthy to ask God for nothing considering the kind of life he lead, but if God could hear from him just one time, Demetrius would beg him to spare his sweet Angel. His voice was hoarse with foreboding as he asked, "She's not dead, is she?"

"No, no, Demetrius. She's not dead, but she's in a bad way. We'll know more after the doctors check her out. I can call you this afternoon with more information if you'd like."

"Don't worry about calling me. I'm on my way. Text me the address to the hospital and I'll rent a car at the airport and drive straight there." He hung up the phone, threw on his shirt and frantically searched for his shoes.

Jasmine had her hands on her hips, foot tapping the floor. "I know you're not rushing out of here like this."

"I've got to go, Jasmine. My wife is in the hospital."

"It's not like one of your kids is in the hospital. This is a woman that you don't even want anymore. You haven't seen her in months."

Demetrius took three twenties out of his wallet and handed them to Jasmine. "I don't have time for this, Jasmine. Get yourself a cab or stay here until check out time. The room has already been paid for."

She threw the money in his face. "Forget you, Demetrius. You're not going to treat me like some two-bit hooker." Then she tried to slap him.

Demetrius grabbed her arm and roughly pulled her close to him. "Look, I don't know what your problem is, but I don't play these kind of games. I don't like putting my hands on women, but if you don't get out of my way I will break your neck and then send one of my men in here to cut you up into so many pieces that they will never find all of you."

He let her go and Jasmine didn't say another word as Demetrius put his shoes on and then left the hotel room.

The whole plane ride to Winston-Salem, Demetrius kept asking himself, what in the world he'd been thinking, getting involved with Jasmine. He wasn't that guy… In the eleven years that he'd been married, he'd never wanted to cheat on Angel. He loved his wife, loved his kids. He didn't want his marriage to end… it was this baby that was ruining everything for them. And now Angel was in the hospital clinging to life because of some kid that he didn't even want anyway.

If his wife was unconscious when he reached the hospital, then he was going to find a doctor who would agree to abort that unwanted fetus and be done with this nightmare once and for all. Then his family could come back home and he and Angel could get back to where they had once been.

~~~~~

"Girl, you gave us a scare," Pastor Barnes said as he and the boys walked into Angel's hospital room.

Angel was now conscious and smiling at the group. "It's not my fault, Daddy. This baby wants to be born before his due date… Give me a break, kid," Angel rubbed her belly. "It's not like you can start the assignment God has for you on day one."

Maxine touched Angel's stomach and lowered her head to talk to the baby. "That's right, there's no rush, little one. Believe me, the world will still be full of sinners by the time you're ready for ministry."

"Thank you, Mama. Please please help me stop this baby from trying to tear his mother's insides apart," Angel tried to get through to her anxious baby. But right now her legs were in stir-ups, with her bottom lifted upward in an attempt to keep the baby from slipping out.

"How long do you have to lay like that, Mama?" DeMarcus asked.

"I'm not sure. Hopefully, this baby will relax and let me get some rest some time soon."

"I'm going to punch him in the nose," Dontae gave his eight year old solution to the problem.

Everyone started laughing, but Dee jumped out of his seat and ran towards the door. Angel turned to see what her son was doing and that's when she saw her husband standing in the doorway looking like the odd man out.

"Daddy, I knew you'd come." Dee wrapped his arms around his father's. Demetrius hugged his son so tight the boy had to push away from him. "Too tight."

"Sorry about that son, I've been missing you."

Dee grabbed his father's hand and marched him into the room.

Angel told him, "We've missed you too."

Maxine moved from her spot next to Angel's bed so Demetrius could sit down.

"What is all of this?" He pointed at the stir-ups and then sat down next to his wife and laid his head on her chest for a long moment without saying another word. She put her hand on his head and rubbed her fingers through his hair. This was her man... her love. Demetrius would come to his senses and they would work through their petty differences. Angel was sure of it.

Pastor Barnes cleared his throat and stood up. "Let's give these two some privacy. Y'all come on, me and your grandmother will take y'all to get a bite to eat."

When the room cleared, Demetrius lifted his head and stared at his wife.

"You didn't say anything to my parents," she reminded him.

"I wasn't trying to be rude. I just saw you in this get up." He pointed at her legs in the stir-ups again, "and my mind went back to DeMarcus' words when he called me a few hours ago and I guess I just couldn't focus."

Grinning at him, she said, "I'm sure they'll forgive you."

"What happened, Bae? DeMarcus said there was a lot of blood in your bed."

Angel patted her belly. "This baby wants to greet the world before his time I guess. He's been trying to kick his way out for a couple of months now."

"I knew you should've had that abortion. What if this baby kills you, then what are me and the boys supposed to do?"

"Don't be angry Demetrius. There's nothing I can do about how hard this pregnancy has been. We've just got to let it run its course."

He stood up and paced the room. When Demetrius turned back to her, he told her honestly, "I don't want to let it run its course. I want your legs out of whatever this contraption is and I want this baby to come out... hopefully, he'll lose oxygen on the way out and won't survive the delivery."

Angel's eyes widened as her hand went to her mouth. "How can you say that? This baby is a life and he is meant to do great things for the Lord. So, you and nobody else can stop God's plan... not this time."

"God's plan? What are you talking about woman? What kind of plan would God have for a child conceived in rape?"

Angel shook her head. "You don't know that. This baby could just as well belong to you and me, and I will give my life to protect him. Do you hear me, Demetrius? I would give my life for this child, just as I know you would give your life for me and our other children."

Demetrius shook his head. "I can't let you do this, Angel. I'm going to talk with the doctors, and if there is any risk to your life, then we are doing to this baby what should have been done months ago."

Tears streamed down Angel's face as Demetrius stormed out of her hospital room. He was so full of hate these days that she barely recognized the man she fell in love with. "Lord please, help Demetrius find the strength in his heart to love this child just as much as he loves our other children.

"This baby belongs to You, God. So, You have got to help my son. His life has been under attack from the moment he was conceived. But You, oh Lord, can help my baby to have a good life. That's all I want for him. Please Lord, Jesus, please help my baby. In Jesus name I pray."

"Them parents of yours got you calling on the name of Jesus?" Demetrius asked as he walked back into the room. He didn't look happy.

"My parents had nothing to do with it."

"Humph." Demetrius' lips twisted. "As soon as this doctor shows back up, I'm getting you released from this hospital and we are going home. This whole thing has gotten out of hand. I'm not going to have you praying as if we need some crutch to lean on."

Angel had wanted to tell Demetrius about her faith each time she talked to him on the phone. But he was still so upset about the baby, that she didn't have the nerve to fess up about being a Christian. It wasn't right. She wasn't ashamed of her Lord. So, from this moment forward she was going to let her light shine. "Sit down for a minute

Demetrius. I need to tell you everything that happened to me the day I was supposed to abort our baby."

Five

"No," was Demetrius' answer to Angel's declaration of salvation. Before he married her, he'd told her that he didn't want anything to do with God, Jesus or His Precious Holy Ghost. But now that they've been married over ten years, Angel thought she could give her life to God and he would just have to roll over and take it. But he wasn't built like that. Demetrius decided he would handle his wife and her Jesus explosion in due time.

Grinning, while trying not to laugh, Angel told him, "You can't just say no and expect my love for God to disappear."

Shaking his head, Demetrius slammed his fist against the wall. "You took vows with me, Angel. And before that, you promised that you'd never go all Jesus freak on me. Do you remember that, Angel? We had an agreement."

"You act like it's the end of the world, Demetrius. I'm still the same person. But now, I have love in my heart for the Lord, what's so wrong with that."

"I'm not going to have you up in my house judging me and acting like you're so much better than me."

"It's our house, Demetrius. Or have I been away so long that you've forgotten that we're a team?"

"I haven't forgotten." Demetrius sat back down next to his wife's bed and frowned as he looked at her legs in those stir-ups again. "But it looks to me like you care more about this baby than you do about our family and the life we've built together. You and me, against the world, Angel... the world we built used to mean something."

She was crying again, because he just didn't get it. "It still does, Demetrius. I love you with all my heart. Don't you know that by now?"

"You just gave God your heart, so I'm no longer the one who matters most. I may not go to church, Angel, but I know how this stuff works, and I'm not having it. Either you're with me or you're with God," he pointed at her belly, "and this kid."

When she didn't respond, Demetrius backed away from his wife, sucked in air through his nose and then told her. "I'm taking our children back with me. You've got two days to make up your mind. Either you're going to come home with me and the kids or stay here with your legs in the air."

"Demetrius, this is our child. Why can't you see this the way I see it. This baby is a blessing from God."

He walked out of the room without saying another word to her. Angel wished she could have ran after her husband... wished she could have found the words to make him understand, help him to see the truth that was staring them in the face. But Demetrius had closed his mind to the possibility of anything other than his way. Angel prayed that he hadn't also closed his heart to her and this baby.

~~~~

Demetrius wanted to throw the visiting room chairs through the window... grab a couple of guys and knock their heads together. Something, anything other than the nothing he was doing right now. How in the world did his father expect him to become the head of the family business when he couldn't even control what was happening with his wife?

Angel had obviously lost her mind. She couldn't be thinking clearly, choosing some mystical God in the sky and a baby that he'd made it abundantly clear he didn't want. Was she trying to force his hand? Did she want him with other women? Because if that's what she wanted, then he could make that happen. And not with Jasmine, that girl didn't know her place. But he could find some women who weren't all Holy Ghost filled and wanted to make him their number one priority.

His cell phone rang. Demetrius saw that it was Al, so he stepped outside the hospital and answered. "Yeah, what's up?"

"Boy, where you at?"

"I'm in Winston-Salem. Angel is in the hospital."

Al hesitated. "I'm sorry to hear that. Is she okay?"

"What do you need?" The last thing Demetrius wanted to talk about was his wife right now.

"It's business, but if you're busy with the family... I can handle it."

"You don't just handle things without talking to me. I'm the head of the business. Remember?"

"Alright. Well, Little Mark is a thief. This is the third time he's shorted us. And he never would have done no mess like this if your daddy was still running thangs."

Demetrius' eyes crossed. He was so sick of hearing how great Don Shepherd was and how men feared him, but they didn't have the same kind of fear for Demetrius. "What would you normally do in a situation like this?"

"You already know what I'd do... and what your daddy would do too for that matter."

"Then this was a conversation we didn't need to have... Oh and Al, don't call me boy again." Demetrius hit the end button, knowing full well that he had just commissioned the killing of another man, and at that moment, he didn't even care.

~~~~

"Why are you crying? What's got you so upset?" Maxine asked as she stepped back into Angel's room.

Angel tried to wipe the tears from her eyes, but they just kept coming. "I don't want the boys to see me like this. Can you tell dad to take them home?"

"Demetrius ran into us as we were coming back to the room. He told your dad that he was taking them to the hotel with him. Demetrius and your dad were making arrangements to get some clothes for the boys when I walked away from them." Maxine grabbed the tissue box off the table and handed it to Angel.

Angel pulled a few tissues from the box, wiped her face and then blew her nose. "He acts like I'm destroying our family, when all I'm doing is having our baby. I just don't get him."

"It sounds like you and Demetrius are in two different places concerning the baby. You see him as a gift from God, but Demetrius doesn't."

"The only thing Demetrius can think about is that this baby could be Frankie's. He'd rather I stop trying to save my baby's life and just let him die, than to wait and see if this is his child or not. And I don't understand how he could feel that way."

Angel cried some more, while Maxine rubbed her arm trying to calm her. "It's not good for you to get this upset. You've got to calm down, honey."

"He's taking my kids back to Dayton. He says that if I don't ask the doctor to release me from this hospital and come home with them, then that means I'm choosing God and this baby over our family.

44

When Maxine didn't respond to that, Angel said, "Say something Mama. I don't know what I should do."

Maxine shook her head. "I can't make this decision for you, Angel. All I can tell you is that the bible says, 'choose for yourself this day, whom you will serve'."

"I want to serve God. I've learned that I can't live without Him and expect to have peace in my life. But Demetrius is going to take my kids. He blames me, when he should be blaming his father. Don is responsible for everything we are going through. And now he wants me to leave town with them, when he knows that if I'm not careful, I could lose this baby."

"Do you trust God?"

As Angel closed her eyes another tear pressed its way through and drifted down her cheek. She wanted to trust that God would change Demetrius' mind and help him to see things the right way, but what if that never happened. She admitted to her mother what she was feeling, "What if he stops loving me?"

"Do you really think that Demetrius could ever stop loving you?

Angel was so thankful that her mother hadn't said, "I told you so". Because Maxine had warned her about being unequally yoked and that the bible asks the question, 'how can two walk together if they do not agree'? Right now, with what Angel was dealing with, that seemed like a really good question.

"I can't answer your question, Mama. Because I really don't know. After all that has happened, and the way Demetrius has responded to this baby and me giving my life to Christ... "I hate to admit it, but I'm scared that he just might stop loving me."

Maxine shook her head. "Don't give up hope, hon. You got to have faith in your man and in your marriage. When your dad messed up and I divorced him back when you and your brother were just kids, I had no idea the trials and tribulations this family would go through before everything was put back right. Let God be God in your marriage… even when it looks like there's no hope, keep looking to God. Do you hear me?"

"Mama, do you remember how you warned me not to marry Demetrius. You said that we came from two different worlds and that we would eventually have problems. I heard every word you said that day, but I truly never saw this coming. I thought Demetrius and I would always be happy."

"The two of you have been through a lot, Angel. Give him time to get to where you are, okay? In the book of Hebrews it says, "*Without faith it is impossible to please Him: for he that cometh to God must believe that He is, and that He is a rewarder of them that diligently seek Him.*"

Angel lay there for a long moment taking her mother's words in. She always liked how her parents were able to recite chapter and verse even without having the actual bible in their hands. Because they had given their lives over to God and in so doing had become walking bibles, being read by men daily. Angel let out a deep sigh, that was almost like a moaning, groaning in her spirit. With tears running down her face, she said, "I've made my choice. From this day forward I choose God and I will trust Him to keep my family together."

Six

Demetrius had given Angel an ultimatum that he meant to make good on... two days to get her priorities straight. She would have to decide what was more important to her? Her family or some other man's baby? Today was the day that he would find out. He was going to ask the doctor to discharge his wife and if she objected... he and the kids would be gone.

His cell phone rang, Demetrius glanced at the caller ID, and it was Angel again. He sent the call to voicemail. He wanted his wife to feel what life without him would be like, so she could come to her senses and make the right choice. He was tired of all her drama about a baby he didn't even want. If Angel loved him, she would understand where he was coming from and just let it go. Let this baby go, so they could move on with their lives and forget about how another man touched his wife in a manner that only he should have been able to do.

This baby would be a constant reminder to Demetrius of not just the attack Angel endured, but of the fact that he hadn't been able to protect her. All these years of being involved in his father's crime family, the one thing that Demetrius took pride in was that he looked out for his family first and made sure nothing that he or his father did came back on his wife or his children.

But while he'd been laid up in jail for something his father had done, his wonderful father had convinced Angel to seek out her ex-boyfriend and ask him for the money needed to post bond. Angel had only agreed to meet with Frankie Day after Don had made it seem like Demetrius was being attacked behind bars and was likely to be murdered.

Don's lie had cost the entire family dearly. Now Demetrius had to find a way to forgive his wife for not only the baby, but for all this Jesus stuff as well. And in his heart Demetrius knew that if it hadn't been for this baby, his wife would have kept her promise to him and left all that God stuff alone. That was something else Demetrius could blame his father for. So when his cell rang again and it was Al telling him that his father had just cut a deal with the feds which ensured that his father and Stan, his father's second in command, would get their sentences reduced from life without parole to ten years, Demetrius couldn't even celebrate with Al over the good news.

"Whassa matter with you, kid. I just told you that your daddy won't be spending the rest of his life in prison and you act like I just told you that McDonald's is now selling chicken sandwiches."

"I've got a lot on my mind, of course I'm happy that dad won't die in prison."

"He'll be seventy when he gets out, but that old dog will still be able to hunt, trust that," Al said.

Demetrius could hear the smile on Al's face. It amazed him how Don, Stan and Al were still thick as thieves after all these years of being friends… more like brothers. They had lost Joe-Joe last year, but they seemed to grow even closer for having to bury one of their own. Demetrius didn't have bonds like that with any of the guys he grew up with. The closest relationship he'd ever had was with Angel. He sighed. "I'll hit you back later, Al. I've got things to do."

He then woke his children up and took them to breakfast. He had truly missed his boys running around the house, breaking up everything in sight and then lying and pointing fingers at each other.

"Are we going to the hospital?" Dontae asked as he wolfed down his pancakes.

"Yep, and then we're going home today, right?" Demetrius reminded his boys.

"But Dad, how can we go home with Mom in the hospital?" Dee wanted to know.

"I've got a feeling that your mother will be released today. She's going to fly back home with us. Won't that be great?"

"Yay!" the boys cheered in unison.

But when they got to the hospital, Demetrius discovered that his plan was about to change.

~~~~

Late last night, Angel had started having contractions. She'd tried calling Demetrius, but he hadn't answered his phone. Her mother and father had arrived at the hospital at about six in the morning, and had been helping her deal with the pain that was ripping through her body.

Demetrius and the kids walked into the delivery room at about ten that morning, just as Angel thought she wouldn't be able to take another gut wrenching, awful contraction, her husband's face appeared before her. He held onto her hand as she screamed. He rubbed her back when she moaned.

Angel was in and out of consciousness as the pain ripped through her body. At one point she heard Demetrius yelling at the doctors. "Why is she in labor? I thought you were trying to avoid this."

"Her stress level is very high, sir. Once the contractions started, we didn't think it was in her or the baby's best interest to stop it."

"Forget the baby, y'all better not kill my wife up in here. I know that."

Angel squeezed Demetrius' hand trying to calm him as he threatened the doctor, the nurses and the hospital in general if anything happened to her. "Bae, calm down, God has got this. The baby will survive." As she said this, she passed out.

Maxine jumped up, with hands lifted to the Most High, she called out, "Jesus! Oh Jesus! My child needs You right now. Help her Lord. See her through this delivery. Let Angel and this baby survive."

Demetrius swung around and angrily told Maxine. "Stop praying for this baby. I just want my wife alive. So if your God is so great, have Him do that for us."

Angel's eyes fluttered as she regained consciousness. She took a deep breath, the pain was unlike anything she'd experienced the three other times she'd given birth. But Angel believed in her heart that God had a plan for this baby and she hoped and prayed that she was also part of the plan. Because she wanted to live to see her child step into the ministry God destined for him. What a glorious day that would be.

But before any of that could come to pass she would have to get her husband to stop being so angry. "Demetrius, I'm okay. This will all be over in a little while. You'll see. I'm going to survive this delivery and then the six of us are going to be a family."

His lip tightened at her 'the six of us' comment, but Demetrius held onto Angel's hand none-the-less. "Just finish this already, Angel. I don't like seeing you in so much pain."

With Demetrius holding onto her hand, Angel was prepared when the next pain hit, she pushed and pushed again.

"I see the head," the doctor told them.

Angel bared down and pushed again.

"You can do this, Angel. Just push one more time and get this job done." Demetrius was sounding like a coach as he encouraged Angel to push one more good time.

When another contraction hit, Angel did exactly as her husband coached and the baby slid out. Angel didn't even wait to see the umbilical cord being cut. She drifted off to sleep with the look of peace over her face.

When Angel opened her eyes again, the room had been cleared out. Her parents were gone. The children weren't there, only Demetrius was left, sleeping by her bed side. She nudged him awake. Demetrius popped his head up.

"Where's the baby?" Angel asked.

"He's in the nursery. I didn't think it was a good idea to let him stay in here with us since we'll be signing the adoption paperwork tomorrow."

"What adoption? What are you talking about, Demetrius." Angel lifted herself into a sitting position. She grimaced and then Demetrius adjusted the pillow behind her back.

"I get it," Demetrius told her. "You didn't want to kill the baby. I can respect that. But now that you delivered this kid, it's time for us to get back to being us, with our three children."

Her voice was calm, but firm. "We have four children now, Demetrius. And I think we should be talking about what to name this baby rather than thinking about ways we can throw him away."

"Look Angel, I don't want to fight with you. I just watched you almost die trying to bring a life into this world that I don't even want. But I'm telling you, right here and now, that I still want my family… I still want you. So, don't ruin what we have."

"Your father ruined what we have. Blame him, not our baby," she yelled at him, trying to make him see reason. All of this was Don's fault, and even though Angel had given her life to the Lord, she doubted that she would ever be able to forgive that man for sending her on a mission of destruction.

"I know my father ruined us, I'm trying to set things back right. We don't need this baby, Angel. Life was good for us before you got pregnant."

"Right before I got pregnant you were begging me to have another child, don't you remember that, Demetrius?"

He nodded. "I remember it. I wanted a little girl and I still do. She'd look just like her mother with big beautiful brown eyes. She'd have cute little pony tails and she'd ask me to play jump rope and hop scotch with her. And I'd do it all. I would even sit down and have a tea party with her... take her to father, daughter dances."

"That's sounds wonderful, Demetrius. And I believe you'd do everything you just said. But what I can't understand is why you wouldn't be there for this baby the same way you've been there for our other sons."

"Because he's not my son!" Demetrius exploded.

"You don't know that, and I'm not going to let you throw him away. So, if you don't want to name him with me, then I'll do it myself."

"What are you saying, Angel? Would you really take this baby over our family? Because that baby is not coming into my house."

"Our house."

"You know what I mean. I'm not sharing space with that... that kid who has ruined everything for us."

"He hasn't ruined anything. You have allowed your father and Frankie to ruin things for us. But I'm not going to live my life like that. I chose to forgive them for what they did. That is the only way that I can be free of it. And as for our son. You don't know that he's not yours. But we can find out with one of them DNA tests I heard about. Why don't we do that?"

Shaking his head, Demetrius stood. "You think I want people knowing that you just had a child that's not mine. That's crazy. No, I'm not doing that."

"And I'm not giving our child up for adoption."

Demetrius looked as if he wanted to slam his fist into a wall. Instead he just stomped out of the room without saying another word.

Angel didn't care that her husband had just stormed out of her room. She hit the nurse button and asked them to bring her baby into the room.

"I'll be right there," the nurse told her.

But when the nurse entered her room, she did not have the baby with her. She had a wheelchair. "You shouldn't be on your feet right now, so I'm going to help you into this wheelchair."

"Why do I need to get in that? Why can't the baby come in here with me like all my other babies did?"

The nurse told her, "The baby was having trouble breathing on his own, so we have to keep him in an incubator for a while. Nothing to worry about. Sometimes this happens with preemies."

The nurse wheeled Angel down the hall so that she could see her son. He looked so small and bruised, like he'd already endured more heartache than one child should endure in a lifetime. His name tag had Shepherd as the last name and baby as the first.

At this point Angel thought it fitting to name the child Jabez, because he was certainly born in pain. But before despair could take hold of her, she reminded herself that her child would grow to be a servant of the Lord. She was determined to give him a name that would be fitting for his future, not his past or present situation.

Seven

Saul, the warrior angel battled long and hard into the night. Legions of warriors were with him and they were just as determined to stop the evil one's mission. When the battle was finished and the war was won Saul looked up as a door in heaven opened and a voice that sounded like thunder and lightning said, "Come up hither."

Saul was immediately transported from the earthly realm into the heavens. Saul found himself standing not far from the throne and the One who sat on it. He that sat on the throne was to look upon like jasper and a sardine stone: and there was a rainbow round about the throne, like an emerald.

Saul immediately fell to his knees in reverence to His Lord as he looked round about the throne to see four and twenty seats: and upon the seats he saw four and twenty elders sitting, clothed in white raiment; and they had on their heads crowns of gold.

Out of the throne proceeded lightings and thunderings and voices: and there were seven lamps of fire burning before the throne, which are the seven Spirits of God. And before the throne there was a sea of glass like unto crystal: and in the midst of the throne, and round about the throne, were four beasts full of eyes before and behind. The first beast was like a lion, and the second beast like a calf, and the third beast had a face as a man, and the fourth beast was like a flying eagle. The four beasts each had six wings about him; and they were full of eyes within: and they rest not day or night, saying Holy, Holy, Holy, Lord God Almighty, which was and is, and is to come.

"Arise," the voice of thunder and lightning told Saul.

Saul stood, but kept his head bowed low. Then he heard the words, he'd been anticipating for years.

"The child is alive."

Saul put his hand on his sword. And then, in an instant he was no longer bowed low before the throne but standing upright in front of Captain Aaron.

Captain Aaron told him, "The wicked one has unleashed an attack on the child that will destroy him if it is not dealt with. You know your mission… it's time to put it in action."

"I've waited years for this, Captain. I won't fail our earthly warrior."

~~~~

Angel named him Obadiah Damerae Shepherd. Both were biblical names. Obadiah meant, servant of God and Damerae meant, boy of joy. She wanted desperately for her little servant of God to know joy, even in the face of those who would hate him without a cause.

Obadiah and Damerae was a mouthful for a little baby who wasn't even six pounds yet and was still in an incubator, even after two weeks. So, Angel took to calling him Dam. Today, when she arrived at the ICU to see Dam, she was greeted with the wonderful news that her son was now breathing on his own and she would be able to hold him.

As the nurse put him in her arms, Angel's heart filled with joy. She wanted to call Demetrius and share the good news about Dam, but she knew it would not sound like music in Demetrius' ears. He was probably hoping that Dam would never learn to breath on his own. Shame on you, Angelica Shepherd, you shouldn't think such terrible things about your husband, even if they are true, she chided herself as the nurse handed her a bottle.

"I get to feed him?" her eyes lit up.

"You sure do?"

Angel couldn't believe this day had come. The day after she gave birth to her son, Demetrius packed up the kids and went back home, not even caring that she and Dam wouldn't be able to travel at that point. That was the lowest day of her life. She'd cried herself to sleep every night since that day. But today was a good day. She was not only holding her son, she was also feeding him. She Looked down at her son as he wrapped his small lips around the nipple of the bottle and greedily sucked on it. She laughed, but as she realized that she didn't have anyone to share this moment with, the laughter caught in her throat. "Well Dam, it's just you and me kid. I'm so glad that we've got God on our side."

Once Dam finished with his bottle, Angel burped him and then took out her bible as she had done each day during their time together. Today she read from Proverbs, chapter three:

"My son, do not forget my law, but let your heart keep my commands; for length of days and long life and peace they will add to you. Let not mercy and truth forsake you; bind them around your neck, write them on the tablet of your heart. and so find favor and high esteem in the sight of God and man.

Trust in the Lord with all your heart, and lean not on your own understanding; in all your ways acknowledge Him, and He shall direct your paths. Do not be wise in your own eyes; fear the Lord and depart from evil. It will be health to your flesh, and strength to your bones."

Angel kept coming to the hospital reading the word of God to her son and waiting for the day that he would be released. She didn't understand why her son was going through so much, at such a young age. She only prayed that life would become like a sweet melody for him, and that he wouldn't remember anything of how his life began,or how his father rejected him. She prayed that her love would be enough for Obadiah Damerae Shepherd.

The next month and the month after that was hard for Angel. She missed her other three boys, but Dam had stayed in the hospital for six weeks and once he was able to come home with Angel, he still needed a lot of tender loving care. She couldn't quite leave him yet, so that she could visit her other children. And Demetrius wasn't making things any easier on her. Calling every other day and demanding that she come home to take care of his children, while completely ignoring their other child.

Then Demetrius would put the kids on the phone, and Angel would cry every time she heard their voices begging her to come home. But once her husband was back on the phone and she would agree to come home with Dam, Demetrius would tell her over and over that Dam was not allowed in *his* house.

Looking to heaven Angel asked, "What should I do, Lord. I'm caught in the middle and I don't have answers for anybody."

~~~~

Maxine and Marvin were out to dinner trying to enjoy a date night that was long overdue, but even with steak and lobster on their plates, they couldn't seem to get their minds off of Angel's dilemma.

"I just don't understand why Demetrius is giving her such a hard time. Dam is a wonderful baby, he should be honored to have this child."

"It's his pride, Maxine. In his mind this child represents his wife being with another man. And the worst part of all is that she was raped by that man. Someone like Demetrius takes pride in protecting his family. But he couldn't protect Angel."

"Okay, but Angel isn't blaming him. She has moved on, and thank God, she now has put her trust in the Lord. I don't know how she would be able to get through all of this drama if she hadn't." Maxine was hot, she wanted to fly to Ohio and shake some sense in Demetrius' thick head.

Marvin took his wife's hand. "Let's pray over our food and at least try to enjoy our night out."

Maxine bowed her head as her husband said grace over their food. She then tried to enjoy her dinner. She was out on the town with her man… the one who'd almost got away because they had been too young and immature to accept the call of God on their lives without letting it go to their heads. Or better yet, her husband had been the one to let all the people calling him the greatest pastor who ever lived go to his head.

Women started propositioning him without regard for the fact that he had a wife. Marvin had put them in their place at first, but as his head continued to swell, he stopped putting women in their place, and allowed them to take more and more of Maxine's place.

Maxine had gotten fed up and divorced her husband. But years later, she was able to see firsthand how God had turned Marvin into a man who could be trusted… a man after God's own heart. Maxine was then able to give him her heart again. They had gone down a hard road… one that she didn't want Dam to go down once he accepted his call to the ministry. So, she stayed in prayer for her grandson.

At times, Maxine chided herself because she was now praying for Dam more than she was praying for her other grandchildren. She didn't know if that was God's plan or if she just felt so sorry for Dam that she was over praying for him… she didn't even know if that was a thing. Could you over pray for a person?

"Honey, did you hear anything I said?" Marvin asked, as he took the last bite of his steak.

She smiled at him. He was still the handsomest man she knew. "I'm sorry. I know I shouldn't be so distracted, but really I am."

"I'm distracted too, so if you don't want to go to the movies, I'll understand."

"Why don't we go home and watch a movie," Maxine suggested.

Marvin paid the check and took his wife home.

They tried to watch a movie but Maxine's eye lids felt so heavy that she drifted off to sleep about halfway through. In her dream she found herself walking down a long corridor. As she reached the end, she opened the door, inside the room she saw her daughter pregnant and giving birth again. That was the last thing Maxine wanted to see, because Angel's labor had been so hard that Maxine never wanted her to go through that again. But she evidently had come into the room at the end of the labor. Angel pushed and the baby slid out.

Demetrius then helped Angel off the bed and she walked out of the room with him. Maxine started to call after her daughter, but then a man with holes in his hands picked up the baby, wrapped him in brilliantly colored cloth of many colors and then handed him to her.

Maxine looked down at the baby, trying to figure out why she had him in her arms. He was so small that she worried that she could hurt him. But right before her eyes he began to grow. She glanced over at the man who'd handed the baby to her, his face was shaded, so she couldn't see it, but those hands... she saw and recognized them.

Still holding the baby, Maxine bowed down and said, "My Lord."

The Lord said to her, "The child needs you. You shall help raise him up." and then the Lord was gone.

Maxine sat up and looked around the room, trying to figure out where she was. When she recognized her surroundings, and realized that she was at home in her bed, she relaxed. But then a thought hit her. It was time for Angel to go home, and she and Marvin would need to raise Dam for a little while.

Saul smiled as Maxine caught everything he dropped into her spirit. His job was done for now, but Dam had a long way to go before he could walk into his ministry. Saul would be back.

Eight

"You really think that God wants you to take care of Dam so I can go home and take care of my other children?" Angel couldn't believe what her mother was saying. How could she just leave her baby?

"This is the way it must be for now, honey. But I don't believe that this is forever… this is more like a bit of a respite for Dam. Your father and I will continue to teach him the word of God and raise him as if he is indeed meant to go into ministry as you, yourself told us."

"But Mama…" Angel began, but Maxine put a hand on her shoulder.

"I know this is hard, Angel, but we have got to trust God. Can you do that?"

Angel closed her eyes, and took a deep breath. "I'm having a hard time with my faith right now, Mama, and I just don't know what to do about it."

"What are you having trouble with? Do you mind talking about it?"

Sighing deeply, Angel said, "I have so much unforgiveness in my heart for how Demetrius has treated me and Dam. We didn't cause any of this. He should be blaming his awful father for all of this. But instead he's taking it all out on us."

"It sounds like you have some unforgiveness in your heart for Demetrius' father also."

Angel didn't bother to deny it, she nodded. "I do. What does that say about me and my Christianity?"

"It says that you're human, honey. Look, most Christians face hardships or had something done to them that has caused bitterness to enter their hearts. But bitterness only allows Satan to steal your joy, so your dad and I will be praying that one day, you find the strength to forgive."

~~~~

It was hard for Angel to accept, but her mother finally convinced her that she should go back to Dayton to see about her other children and leave the baby in her care. If it wasn't for the fact that Dam was doing so much better, Angel didn't think she would have been able to pull herself away from the child. She was also thankful for her parents' prayers because seeing Demetrius again after the stuff he tried to pull at the hospital was a real test.

Demetrius picked her up from the airport and drove her to their new home. A place she hadn't spent one day in or picked one piece of furniture for. Even before she reached the house, Angel knew that some things had changed, and that she wasn't going to like the changes to her lifestyle.

There was a security gate, with a security guard on duty. Demetrius used a card key to gain entry into this massive, monstrosity of a house that Angel doubted she'd ever be able to clean."

"How on earth are we able to afford all of this, Demetrius? And why so much security?"

"You think I'm going to let another one of my father's enemies burn our house down again?"

"You never explained all of that to me. So, the house burning down wasn't an accident just as I suspected?" Angel watched the lines on Demetrius' forehead grow. A sure sign that he didn't want to discuss this with her.

"Let's just get you in the house so you can get settled. The boys have missed you and as soon as they get out of school, they'll be running in here looking for you."

She had missed her boys as well. So, Demetrius was right. They could discuss all these changes later. She wanted to find their bedroom, take a quick nap and then greet her children for the first time in three months.

Unfortunately, the greeting with her sons was not the heartwarming experience Angel imagined it to be because just as her sons were hugging and kissing her and telling her how much they missed her a scantily dressed woman stepped out of the driver's side of the car the boys had just exited. She walked right up to Demetrius, kissed him on the cheek and then handed him the keys.

Angel then told her boys, "Y'all go into the house. Mama will be right in." Once they closed the door behind them, Angel pointed at the woman standing next to Demetrius as if she was laying claims on a man that didn't belong to her. "Who is this?"

"Don't start trippin', Angel. You decided to stay with your parents while the boys and I came back here. Of course I had to hire help to take care of them."

"Help don't kiss you on the cheek, Demetrius. I'm not a fool and I won't be treated like one either." Angel was so angry that she lifted her hand and slapped Demetrius for what he had done to them. Here she was, trying to forgive him, but he wasn't worthy of forgiveness.

He stepped back, grabbing her hand so she couldn't hit him again. "Watch yourself, you don't want this fight."

"Oh what are you going to do to me now? Are you going to hit me, because you've done everything else to me? Why not just become a wife beater too?"

The girl stuck her hand out to Angel and said, "I'm Serena Davis. And I really don't think we need to be arguing out here on the front porch. Why don't we go inside and discuss this?"

Angel breathed in, settled herself down, but then she told little Ms. Serena, "If you even think about stepping one foot inside my house, I will have you arrested. Do you hear me?"

"Arrested? But my clothes are in there."

Demetrius spoke up. "She's been staying in the guest room, Angel. Just as KeKe did when she helped you out with the kids."

Angel turned cold eyes on her husband. Her hand went to her hip. "Get this woman off my property or I'm going to pack my kids up and leave. I will not be disrespected by you this way. Not after all I've been through for you." Angel didn't wait for a response from Demetrius. She stomped up the stairs and went into the house, slamming the door behind her.

"Are you okay, Mama?" DeMarcus asked.

She tried to calm herself, but she doubted she would be calm anytime soon. "I'm okay. Mama just needs a little rest. I'm going to take a nap," even though she had just finished taking a nap, "and then I'll come back down here with you and your brothers." She then ran up the stairs trying to get to her room before the tears started falling.

Angel couldn't explain it, but the pain she felt at knowing Demetrius had been unfaithful to her was like the pain she felt when Frankie raped her. This man who took vows with her, and promised to love, honor and cherish her was no longer interested in keeping his promises evidently.

Angel cried over the betrayal and heartbreak she was feeling long into the night. Not once did her husband come into the room to check on her or to apologize for allowing that woman into their home. Angel cried even harder over the fact that Demetrius hadn't come to see about her. Cried until she fell asleep.

By the next morning when she awoke and Demetrius was not lying next to her in bed. She threw the covers off and then got down on her knees to pray before she left the room. Angel desperately needed God to give her direction. She didn't want to divorce her husband because she had been a product of divorce and knew first hand how children were harmed when parents split up. But surely God didn't expect her to just take the dirt Demetrius was dishing out.

After praying, Angel put on a house coat and walked around the house in search of her sons. She hadn't spent any time with them at all last night, and she felt terrible about that. It was Saturday morning, so they didn't have to rush off to school. Angel knocked on doors as she tried to figure out which room belonged to which kid. As she found DeMarcus, Dee, and Dontae's rooms she invited each one to come downstairs with her for breakfast.

The house was too big. Angel hadn't been able to work out in months, so getting from one side of the house to the other caused exhaustion. What was the use of having a mansion and security to guard this monstrosity if the people inside it were miserable?

Standing behind the stove, Angel fixed bacon and French toast for her kids. Dee's face lit up. "I'm so glad you're home, Mom. All we've been eating for breakfast is cereal or pop tarts."

"I thought your dad hired someone to look after you all while I was away." Angel knew she was wrong for putting her kids in the middle of this, but she wanted to see if they knew what had been going on in this house.

"Who Serena?" DeMarcus rolled his eyes. "She can't cook. All she did was drive us to our practices and order pizza."

"Are you telling me that you don't like pizza anymore, DeMarcus?" Angel smiled at her oldest.

"I'm not saying that. Let's not get crazy in here. But I am tired of having people drive me around. I should have my own car by now. But dad acts like he's scared I'm going to wreck or something."

"I'm not worried about you, son. You're a good driver," Demetrius said.

Angel hadn't even heard him come into the house, but she knew that he hadn't just entered the kitchen from another room because she watched him place his keys on the counter. "Lord give me strength," she muttered under her breath.

Demetrius continued talking to DeMarcus. "This is a dangerous world, Son. And there are a lot of people out there who have it in for me and your grandfather. I have security around the house. But once you're off-sight, I can't always guarantee that I can protect you. That's why I don't won't you out there driving by yourself."

"We're not the president's kids, Dad. We don't need the Secret Service," Dee chimed in.

"Whattin' nobody talking to you, boy." Demetrius playfully muffed Dee upside the head. "You always running that mouth."

"I'm just sayin'. You're getting paranoid in your old age."

"Paranoid or not, it's my job to keep you all safe." Demetrius then glanced over at Angel and said, "Good morning."

He said 'good morning' as if he'd been outside taking the trash out when she came downstairs. She wanted to scratch his eyes out for staying out all night and then having the nerve to talk to her. But she wasn't going to go off on him in front of her children. "Good morning."

"You got enough French toast for me?"

Good Lord, please help your child. "I'll make you a few slices."

Demetrius sat down at the counter with the kids while Angel handed each of the kids their plates. She then turned back to the stove without saying a word and put Demetrius' French toast on the skillet. With each flip of the toast, a tear dropped. Angel wanted desperately to stop crying, but her heart was broken into so many pieces that she couldn't control it.

Demetrius walked up behind her and whispered in her ear, "The kids are staring at you."

Angel quickly wiped the tears from her face. She placed Demetrius' food on a plate, handed it to him and then disappeared into her room again.

~~~~

Seeing his wife break down like that in front of him and the kids tore at Demetrius' heart. He'd never meant to hurt Angel. From the moment he met her, all he'd ever wanted to do was protect her from the monsters that would seek to harm her. They'd been married almost thirteen years now, most of their marriage had been total bliss; but Demetrius just couldn't get over the terrible things that had happened to them in the last year.

He knew that it wasn't Angel's fault, but the fact that another man touched her and now she wanted him to raise that man's baby, was more than he was capable of doing. Demetrius knew that he'd been seriously acting out. He wanted to stop what he was doing. But he needed Angel to meet him halfway.

"Why is mom crying? Isn't she happy to see us?" Dontae asked as tears now rolled down his face.

"Of course she's happy to see you. She just misses the baby too. That's all. So, I want you boys to be extra nice to your mom. And give her a little time to adjust to being back home with us. Okay?"

"Yeah Dad, we can do that," DeMarcus said, but then he questioned, "Why didn't she bring Dam home with her?"

"Well, the baby still can't travel. He was very sick and needs to stay down there with the doctors who have been treating him," Demetrius lied.

He then went upstairs and lied some more. He opened the bedroom door and saw his wife on her knees, sobbing and calling out to God. He closed the door and rushed to her side. Demetrius pulled her in his arms and tried to wipe away the tears, but they were ever flowing. "I'm sorry baby, I'm so sorry. Please forgive me."

Angel tried to respond but the only sound coming from her was a guttural moaning.

"Stop crying, Bae. I was wrong. I know I was, but I can't take seeing you like this."

"You're destroying us. I wish I could just divorce and be done with it," she told him as the moaning and groaning continued.

"Never." He violently shook his head. "I'll never let go of us. You're my heart, Bae. Just work with me so we can get back to where we used to be." Demetrius was the head of a criminal organization that sent shivers down the spines of most of the dope boys on the street. But right here, right now, he was powerless against the assault of his wife's tears. He'd move heaven and earth to see her smile again. But his wife didn't want heaven and earth, she wanted a child that he wanted nothing to do with. And Demetrius couldn't figure how to cross that divide.

Nine

Demetrius tried to change his ways. He'd told Serena that they were done and had even torn up a telephone number from a woman he'd been planning to hook up with. The only thing he couldn't change was the job that he had to do. He had a meeting with three of his top guys. They were having problems with some of the field soldiers and Al thought they needed to make a statement.

Sammy had been one of his father's street hustlers, but when Demetrius took over, he brought him up in the ranks along with his old friend Mo. Now, Al, Sammy, Mo and Demetrius sat in his office discussing the current struggle.

"I'm telling you, Demetrius, Leon ain't trying to do the right thing. I hear he's buying his stuff from some guy in Atlanta," Mo said.

"And that ain't good for business. Because if the rest of these fools start taking their business to Atlanta, then how are we going to move our product? Are we supposed to go out on the street corners and start slinging rock again?" Sammy asked.

Al shook his head. "That ain't never gon' happen."

"Then what y'all want to do about this problem," Demetrius asked.

"You know what I want to do about it," Al told him.

Demetrius frowned. "We can't put a hit on everybody that doesn't do what we ask, the minute we ask. We need to at least give him a chance to right his wrong." Demetrius turned to Mo. "What you think?"

Mo looked to Al and nodded. "I'm with Al on this one. Leon being all bold about it. He's thumbed his nose at us from day one. He's treating us like some suckas. He never would have done Don like this. You got to do some damage to this one."

Everybody was always telling him what Don wouldn't have put up with or how these hustlers wasn't respecting him the same as they had respected his father. But in truth, it had never been about respect, Don instilled fear in everyone he came into contact with, mostly because he didn't have anything to lose.

Don didn't have three kids and a wife he desperately wanted to protect and keep as far away from the dope game as possible. No, Don threw his only son into the game head first, and just stood back and waited to see whether he'd sink or swim.

Demetrius looked at his watch and then stood. He had to take Angel and the kids to the airport. It was spring break and they were headed to North Carolina. "I'll go with y'all on this one. But we need to hit Leon hard. I don't want a repeat of the war my father put this city through after Joe-Joe died."

~~~~

Angel could see that Demetrius was trying, he'd taken them to the airport, given the kids some pocket money and then kissed her goodbye. But things still weren't good between them because she couldn't act as if Dam didn't exist. And every six weeks when she left town to spend the week with her son, she wondered what Demetrius was up to. Especially this week. It was spring break, so the kids came to North Carolina with her. They were happy to see their brother. They hadn't seen him since the day Angel gave birth to him, because Demetrius had taken them home the very next day.

71

Angel thought it would be good for the kids to come with her so they could spend some time with Dam, but it proved to be the hardest week she'd endured thus far, because once the kids saw Dam and realized that he wasn't sick as Demetrius had told them, the questions started. "Is Dam coming home with us this time?" Dontae asked.

"No baby, he's going to stay here with grandma and papa."

DeMarcus' eyebrows furrowed. "Dam doesn't look sick at all. Why won't the doctors let him come home with us?"

She wanted to tell her boys that their father was this awful man who didn't want to have anything to do with his own son. But she remembered reading in her bible about how wicked the tongue could be. So she tried her best not to lash out and say something that she wouldn't be able to take back. "My mom has agreed to help me with Dam while your dad and I iron out some details. You boys have so many activities that it's hard for me to do it all."

DeMarcus didn't look as if he believed a word she was saying. That was tough for Angel, because she didn't want to lie to her children. And she was being as honest as she could be without coming right out and saying that the issue she and their dad had to iron out was Demetrius' disdain for his own child.

But that wasn't Angel's only heart break that week. As they were leaving, Dam clung to her and cried non-stop for about an hour. He was only five months, but he seemed to understand that his mommy was leaving him… again.

So when Angel got back home with the kids, she was in no mood for her husband. He came up behind her, pulled her into his arms. "I missed you, Baby."

She shrugged away from him and continued taking her clothes out of the suitcase.

He turned her to face him. "What's wrong?"

A bitter sort of laugh escaped her. "Are you serious?"

"Okay, I know," he lifted his hands, backing off a bit. "You get like this for a few days after you come home from your parents' place."

"Why can't you even say it? I'm not just visiting my parents' place. I'm visiting our son. A child whose name you won't even utter."

Demetrius sat down in the chair that had been placed next to the walk-in closet. "I think I know what we need to do to fix this."

Angel was doing her best to ignore him as she continued to unpack.

"We need to have another baby... the little girl that I've always wanted."

She swung around, eyes wide with fury. "Are you insane? What kind of monster have you become?"

Demetrius got up, started walking towards her. "Now just listen to me. Let me explain."

"How dare you think that having another child could ever replace the one that you have denied me? My mother tried to warn me about marry a man like you. But I loved you so much that I never imagined you could ever be so cold hearted and cruel, not just towards me, but to your own child."

"Don't you want to have a little girl with me?"

"Don't you want to be proud of the little boy we already have?" she countered.

Her comment angered him. His lip twisted. "If you're not interested in working on our marriage, then what do you want to do?"

"I'll show you what I want." She walked into the closet and pulled several of his pants and shirts off the hanger and walked down the hall to the guest bedroom and threw the clothes in there.

Demetrius grabbed hold of her arm. "What are you doing?"

"I'm getting you out of my bedroom. I don't want anything else to do with you. Do you hear me, Demetrius Shepherd? If you don't want to acknowledge Dam as your son, then I don't want you."

"He's not my son!"

Angel wasn't about to back down against Demetrius. He was wrong and she wasn't going to act as if everything was just fine and dandy between them. "Let me tell you something Demetrius Shepherd, if you and your father would have gotten yourself normal jobs instead of trying to be kingpins, then you wouldn't have gotten arrested. And I wouldn't have had to go crawling to Frankie for your bail money. So, you can mistreat me and Dam all you want, but don't you ever forget that all of this falls at your feet for constantly lying to me about what type of business you're actually in."

She grabbed another batch of his clothes, but as her anger boiled over, she handed them to him. "You can clear your things out of *my* room yourself. I'm leaving."

"Where do you think you're going? We need to talk."

Angel glared at him and then she just walked away. She never imagined that there would come a day when she didn't even want to be in the same room with the man she vowed to love for a lifetime. But they had reached that point. If it wasn't for her boys, Angel would have gotten herself right back to the airport and flew back to North Carolina to be with Dam.

But her other children needed her too. DeMarcus would be off to college in a couple of years on a football scholarship, as long as he didn't get hurt before that time. And Angel needed to make sure that he picked the right college. Dee and Dontae had their own issues. Dee struggled in school while Dontae was striving in school by reading two levels above his grade. Angel wanted to make sure that all of her boys became successful in life. But she felt stuck.

She drove over to the soul food restaurant that KeKe managed so she could talk with her friend. KeKe was busy, but she made sure Angel had a plate of food to nibble on while she waited on her. When KeKe finally slid into the booth she said, "Is it that bad?"

Angel nodded, "Even worse."

"I'm sorry to hear that."

"I just don't know what to do, KeKe. He refuses to accept our child. I don't think he'll ever let Dam move into the house with us."

"Have you prayed?" KeKe asked her.

"Girl, I've been on my knees so much that I'm wearing out the rug in my bedroom. I don't know what to do. It breaks my heart to say this but, I'm thinking about leaving him."

KeKe looked her in the eye as she said, "I don't think you understood what I meant so I'm going to ask another way... have you prayed for Demetrius?"

Angel's hand went to her chest as she realized that not once in all these months had she ever prayed for her husband or even sought the Lord for what Demetrius might need her to pray for. He'd been so hateful to her and Dam that Angel had somehow decided that he needed to be treated the same way. But that wasn't being Christ-like, and Angel knew it. She just didn't know how to cross the bridge that separated them.

Ten

3 years later - And a Child Shall Lead Them

"What are you doing, Angel. You've been in North Carolina for three weeks. Don't you think you should be home with us?" Demetrius asked his wife.

Times had not been good to Angel and Demetrius. In the past three years they hadn't done much as a family and she had not allowed him back in her bedroom. So, she was sure he had another girlfriend, but Angel didn't care anymore. "Why does it matter to you, Demetrius? "I'm out of your hair, Dam is out of your hair. So, life should be all good for you."

"I never wanted you out of my hair. This has gone too far, Angel. You need to be home with your family."

Angel missed her boys and she doubted she'd be able to stay away from them much longer. DeMarcus would be leaving for college this summer, and from all accounts, he would do a minimum of two years in college, because scouts were urging him to go pro. This would be his last summer at home, and it was important to Angel that all the family be together and show signs of unity while he was there.

But until Demetrius could bring himself to accept Dam, there would be no unity. "I have family here in North Carolina too, Demetrius. He needs me just as much as you all do. And I won't leave him behind. Not this time." This foolishness had gone on way too long and Angel wasn't going to play these games anymore.

Sighing deeply, Demetrius cleared his throat. "Look, maybe for once the two of us can reach a compromise that we both can live with."

"I'm listening," Angel told him.

"I want you home this week. You can bring Dam with you. But I'm moving back into our bedroom and you will have a little girl to complete this family."

"I'm not God Demetrius. I can't just will myself to have a girl. What if it's another boy?"

"Then you'll have another baby until I get my little girl. That's the deal. Take it or leave it, but," Demetrius added, now sounding more like the kingpin he'd grown to be, "if you leave it, then I'm divorcing you. I've had enough. Do you understand what I'm telling you, Angel?"

He didn't scare her. Angel's voice was just as determined as she told him. "I understand perfectly, Demetrius. I need to pray about this and I'll get back with you in a couple of days?"

"Pray about what? You're my wife. I said get home and get to having another baby. That's it. Nothing to pray about."

She heard the anger in his voice and it didn't move her. "I'll give you a call by Friday." She hung up the phone and then went back into the family room to continue playing with Dam's favorite toy, the blocks her mom had special ordered for him. Memory verses were on the blocks and Dam almost had all of them memorized.

The boy was smarter than any three year old she'd ever known. And it fascinated her that Dam hugged on her and loved on her and showed a joy for life that she wouldn't have expected for a little boy who'd basically been abandoned by his parents.

Angel's mom was seated on the sofa reading a book while she and Dam played with the blocks. She made eye contact with her mom and mouthed, "Thank you."

Maxine put the book down. "For what?"

"For taking such good care of Dam. He's just so smart. I don't know how you did it, but I'm grateful."

Maxine laughed. "Girl, I can't take the credit for Dam. This is all God." Maxine then asked Dam to come sit on her lap. When he did, she picked her bible up off the coffee table and told Angel, "Let me show you something."

Angel got off the floor and sat down next to her mother on the sofa.

Maxine placed the bible in front of Dam and said, "Show your Mama your favorite scripture."

Dam took the bible from his grandmother and opened it. He began flipping through the Old Testament, and through the New Testament until he reached the second book of Timothy. He then pointed at several verses and said, "Read it to me again, Granny."

Maxine told Angel, "He picks the same verses every time." She handed her daughter the bible.

Angel took the bible and began reading: "*I charge you therefore before God and the Lord Jesus Christ, who will judge the living and the dead at His appearing and His kingdom: Preach the word! Be ready in season and out of season. Convince, rebuke, exhort, with all longsuffering and teaching. For the time will come when they will not endure sound doctrine, but according to their own desires, because they have itching ears, they will heap up for themselves teachers; and they will turn their ears away from the truth, and be turned aside to fables. But you be watchful in all things, endure afflictions, do the work of an evangelist, fulfill your ministry.*"

As she read, Dam moved out of his grandmother's lap and came to sit on hers. He closed the bible as she read the last word. "That's all, Mama. You can stop reading."

Sometimes, when Angel looked at Dam there was so much fear in her heart for him. Because she didn't understand what God was doing with her son or if this ministry Dam was supposed to step into would one day cause him to be beheaded like John the Baptist, hung on a cross, like Jesus, or shot inside his own church like some modern day preachers had been. But what Angel did know, was that even if harm was to come to her baby, he would still do the will of God. She could see the conviction in his eyes, even at three years old. There would be nothing she could say or do to stop what was to come for her sweet baby.

"He scares me sometimes, Mama," Angel confessed.

Maxine put a hand on Angel's shoulder. "I'm not going to lie, the spiritual knowledge he seems to have scares me at times too. I just pray that I'm alive to see what God has in store for this little man."

"Why you talking like that, Mama? You're not sick, are you?" Angel's mother had a stroke over a decade ago. She'd recovered from the stroke, but it had left her right leg weakened. Maxine used a cane to keep the pressure off the leg. Angel prayed that watching over Dam hadn't been too much of a hardship on her all these years.

"No hon, I'm not sick. Just facing reality. Your father and I are getting up there in age. So, I don't know how many more years we have left on God's green earth."

Angel hadn't planned to talk to her mom about her phone call with Demetrius until she had a chance to pray about it. But now that she mentioned she was getting up there in age, Angel wondered if keeping Dam was proving to be too much for them. Her parents should be enjoying their lives, traveling and spending time with each other.

"Mama, Demetrius wants me to come home."

"Well, he's your husband. I'm sure he's missing you."

"I doubt he misses me. I'm sure he has a girlfriend by now."

"Angel! I had no idea things were that bad between you and Demetrius. The last time he was here, your dad and I prayed for the two of you all night because we could see how much he loves you. But he's got so much hatred in his heart, we feared that hate would win out over love."

"It hasn't been good." Angel wiped a tear from her face. "I don't even know if I want to go home. But he's threatening to divorce me if I don't. And the truth is, I don't even know if I care enough to fight a divorce."

"I'm so sorry to hear that."

"It's been terrible being around him these last few years. I don't know how much more I can take." Angel wiped at her eyes again.

Dam hugged Angel. "Don't cry Mama. I love your smile."

It was no surprise to her that he could make her smile, after all, his middle name meant 'boy of joy'. Obadiah Damerae Shepherd was truly something special. She only wished her husband felt the same way about this little boy. She hugged him back as she said, "Thank you, Dam. Mommy loves your smile too." Then she pointed at his puzzle. "Play with your blocks, baby. Let Mommy talk to granny for a minute."

Dam climbed down and went back to his favorite toy. Then Angel turned to her mother and whispered. "Demetrius said I can bring Dam home with me this time."

Maxine's eyes widened in surprise. "Demetrius is finally ready to be a father."

Angel shook her head. "I don't think that's it, unfortunately. He wants me to agree to have a little girl. But I don't know if I want another child with him. But then again, I can't leave Dam on you until he's eighteen. You and dad deserve some time to yourselves."

"Don't you worry yourself about me and your daddy, Dam has been no trouble at all." Maxine glanced over at her grandson who was busily reciting the words on his blocks. "But I will tell you that Dam misses you so much each time you go home. There have been nights when I've laid with him until he cried his self to sleep."

The knowledge of Dam's pain stung. Angel got up. "I need to pray. I think I'll go to my room now."

~~~~

Demetrius didn't understand it. His wife acted as if she hated him. She didn't want him near her. Look, but don't touch had been the theme of their lives together for the last few years. He now commanded respect on the street, but he wasn't getting an ounce of it in his own house. He'd tried to reason with Angel, but she wasn't interested in being reasonable.

Truth be told, he didn't want another woman, but Angel just kept pushing him away. He could count on one hand the number of times they'd slept together in three years and he'd had to beg like a dog for that. Angel had promised to love and honor him, but Demetrius didn't think the woman even liked him.

If bringing Dam to their home would get things back to normal, then he was finally willing to do it. But, Demetrius wasn't kidding, his demands would have to be met also. It was either that, or this love affair that started fourteen years ago was over. One single act by a devious man had broken his family, now Demetrius only hoped that his concession would be the act that put the pieces back together again.

Mo came into his office, sat down across from him and put his feet up. "What you know good?" a phrase Mo normally used when greeting his boss.

Demetrius shook his head. "Don't have much to tell you, Bro."

"Come on," Mo took his feet down from the desk. "You got money, good kids and a beautiful wife, but you always moping around here lately."

"I'm taking care of it."

"I hope so, because lately your judgement has been off, and you can't afford to be making the wrong decisions out here on these streets."

Demetrius grunted. "Who says my judgement is off? You been listening to Al talk all his trash?"

Mo held up a hand. "Al hasn't told me anything. You and me go way back, Demetrius. So I'm just going to come out and say it."

"Say what?"

"You and I both thought it was foul when Don started dating Leo Wilson's old lady because he was doing business with Leo, and things can get out of hand when you mess with a man's woman."

Demetrius knew that first hand. His woman had been messed with and life had not been the same for them since. "So what are you trying to say, Mo? What is this little lecture all about?"

"Tricia."

"Tricia? Tricia who?"

Mo laughed out loud. "You're kidding right? This is me, Demetrius... I know you like the back of my hand. And I know that you're doing Alejandro's woman."

"And what if I am?" Demetrius became defiant. Nobody told him what to do.

82

"Look, you know I'm the last one to tell a man anything about cheating on his wife... but this thing you got going with Tricia is making it hard for my boys to do business on the street. Alejandro's boys have attacked two of them just within the last week."

"If Alejandro has become a problem, why don't you just take care of the problem?"

Mo shook his head. "We've always done good business with Alejandro. He didn't kill any of our men, he's just trying to send us a message... so do you get it?"

Demetrius leaned back in his seat. He ran his hands over his face. He had never wanted anyone but Angel. Never in a million years had Demetrius imagined that things would turn out the way they had. If Angel didn't come to her senses, he didn't know what he was going to do. Something had to give. "I get you... I'm done with Tricia."

Eleven

On the flight heading home, Angel made sure that Dam was locked into his seat and then she leaned back and closed her eyes. Her parents had done an awesome job with Dam. He loved them, and they loved him. They cried as she left with Dam. Angel knew that they would miss him, but she also felt that they needed time to themselves.

Her parents shouldn't spend their empty nest years raising her child, not when she and Demetrius were able to take care of their own child. Angel believed that if Demetrius was around Dam and saw what a wonderful child he was, that he would finally do right by his son.

After all, her husband was a good man. He'd been good to her. Demetrius had rescued her from an awful man who'd been trying to turn her into a prostitute. And then he'd taken her into his home, even though he had to suffer the wrath of his father for doing it. It had been fourteen years ago, and she still remembered it like it was yesterday...

Slamming his keys down on the counter as he entered his home, Demetrius punched the fridge, letting out his frustration. He then slammed his fist on the counter, he practically growled throughout the house, "I hate him!"

Angel stepped into the kitchen with a worried look on her face. "Is everything alright?"

Demetrius glanced her way, he'd forgotten that he had brought her to his home.

Leaning against the fridge, Angel told him, "If you want me and DeMarcus to get our stuff and leave, it's cool. I appreciate what you did for us. But I don't want to be a burden to anybody."

"Did I say you was a burden?"

"No, but you don't look very happy." Then as she noticed something she rushed to Demetrius 'side and put her hand on his lip. "You've been bleeding. Let me get some ice."

"I don't need no ice."

Ignoring him, Angel took a few ice cubes out of the freezer and wrapped them in the kitchen towel. She placed it on Demetrius' lip, asking, "You got into another fight?"

"I wouldn't call it a fight."

"What would you call it then, because I can tell that you've been in a scuffle?"

Demetrius shrugged. "Just my father's way of saying thanks for costing him five big ones."

Angel's hand flew to her mouth as she dropped the ice she was holding against Demetrius' lip. She bent down to pick up the ice. Dumping the ice in the sink, she said, "I'm so sorry for all the trouble I've caused. But I promise that I will find a way to pay you or your father every cent that I owe."

Demetrius had rescued Angel from Frankie Day, and Angel would forever be grateful for that. Frankie had tried to pimp her out in order to pay a debt that was owed to Don Shepherd. But Demetrius saw that Angel wasn't about that kind of life, and he made sure she never had to deal with Frankie again. Angel hadn't told Demetrius that she was coming home today so she caught a cab to the house. When the security guard looked inside the cab, he waved at Angel as he lifted open the gate. But before the cab driver could move forward, the security guard pointed at Dam and asked, "Got family visiting?"

"This family member is staying. He is our son," Angel answered while ignoring the puzzled look on the guards face.

"Who's that man, Mama?" Dam asked as they drove up to the house.

"He works for your father. He guards the house and keeps us safe." Angel prayed that Dam would never figure out why they needed to be kept safe. She wished she didn't know, but you could only be blind for so long.

She paid the cab driver and then she and Dam went inside. "Mama this house is big."

"You'll get used to it once you start running around here with your brothers. Come on, let me take you to your room so you can take a nap."

"No nap," Dam complained.

"Naps are good for you, don't you remember what Grandma Maxine said."

"Naps help me to grow big and strong."

"That's right baby." She left their suitcases by the front door, picked Dam up and headed upstairs. The bedroom next to DeMarcus' room was the smallest of the bedrooms, so none of the boys had wanted it. Last year, Angel had purchased a twin size bed for the room. She took Dam to his room and laid him down.

As she pulled the covers over his body, Dam asked, "Is my daddy here?"

Angel didn't know what kind of psychological problems Dam would have because of the absence of his father. She only prayed that the love of God would outweigh the love he'd missed from his father. "He'll be home later, baby. Go to sleep, and you'll see him when you wake up."

Angel then went back down the hall toward her bedroom. She needed a hot bath and a nap herself. But as she opened the door to her room, she stopped as her eyes took in her room. Demetrius' shoes were on the floor next to the bed and his clothes were sprawled over the chair. Her husband had moved back into their bedroom, and Angel didn't know how she felt about that. Before she had time to process it, there was a hand on her back.

"I missed you, Bae," Demetrius whispered in her ear. "I hope you at least missed me a little bit."

Angel closed her eyes as she desperately tried to figure out if she had missed her husband. She'd been gone almost a month and she had enjoyed spending every one of those days with Dam. She'd enjoyed going to church with her parents and hanging out with them. She had missed her DeMarcus, Dee, and Dontae... but had she truly missed Demetrius?

"You don't have no words for me?" Demetrius asked as he stepped back to look at her.

"Have you been behaving yourself?"

Demetrius shook his head, clearly not pleased with her question. "Look, I know I messed up by having Tricia in the house."

"Who's Tricia?" Angel eyebrow lifted.

"You know who I mean... Serena... old girl. I had her in the house taking care of the kids because I needed help. But I didn't bring nobody in this house when you left this time, did I?"

"I guess I should thank you or something?" Sarcasm dripped from every syllable of each word she said.

"I'm not trying to fight with you, Angel. I just came in here to tell you that I'm glad your home."

She pointed at his shoes. "Looks like you moved yourself back into my room."

"Our room," he corrected her. "And of course I moved back in. I should have never allowed you to kick me out of here in the first place. We have drifted so far apart since then and I don't like it at all."

Looking around the room, Angel's eyes focused on the bed. She then turned back to her husband and said, "Demetrius, I just don't know if I'm ready to trust you with my heart again. You have broken it into so many pieces, that I'm still trying to put it back together."

"Doesn't your religion say something about forgiving people?"

"You broke my heart and you just want me to let it go, like nothing happened?" She couldn't believe him. He was so insensitive.

"We've been at odds for three years, Angel. Can't we just call a truce and get on with living our lives together?"

Narrowing her eyes at him, she asked, "Why are you trying to sound so reasonable? Didn't you just threaten to divorce me last week?"

"I haven't stopped loving you, Angel. You haven't forgotten what our love felt like have you?" His eyes implored her to tell him something good.

"I haven't forgotten."

Smiling Demetrius pulled her into his arms. "See, that's all I'm saying. You can't just give up on us. We've got to give our love a chance."

Hesitating for a moment, then she sighed as she told him. "Okay, you can stay in the room, but I'm not ready to have make love with you. Considering all that has happened, I hope you can understand that I need a little more time."

Twelve

Angel woke early the next morning, she stared at Demetrius as he laid next to her. They hadn't shared a bed in three years, and she wasn't so sure how she felt about him being here right now. The man had cheated on her, denied their son and totally disrespected her more times than she could count over the last few years, but for some reason, she wasn't ready to say goodbye. Obviously, none of his other women satisfied him, because he was here in their bed even after she had refused to be intimate with him.

She started thinking back on everything they'd been through and how hard it had been to live in his world, especially since she now believed that God's way was the right way. But the love she once had for this man had been so strong, Angel had to believe that it would one day return just as strong. Maybe if she had the little girl he wanted, then Demetrius might give Dam a chance and that would help her heart to grow for him.

Demetrius turned toward her in bed and opened his mouth as he snored. At that moment Angel decided to take matters into her own hands. She slid out of bed and went into the bathroom. She walked over to her sink and opened the drawer. She pulled out a pack of Q-tips and then got back in bed.

He rolled back over and she thought she would have to get out of bed and crouch down on his side of the bed to wait for him to open his mouth again. But just as she was about to throw the covers off and get out of bed, he turned back over. As he faced her his mouth opened with a great big yawn. Angel quickly put the Q-tips in his mouth and rubbed them from the middle of the jaw to the bottom. She pulled it out just as he closed his mouth.

Angel opened her night stand and quickly placed the Q-tips in there. Later that day, she would purchase a DNA kit and mail it off in order to get the proof she needed. Angel then flopped back down on the bed and tried to make herself go to sleep, but all the while she was thinking… it wasn't supposed to be like this. Angel could still remember the day that she and Demetrius made sweet promises to each other and pledged to let nothing tear them apart.

Demetrius and Angel Shepherd laid on the beach gazing into each other's eyes. They had said 'I do' just two days ago and were now enjoying a week-long vacation in the Bahamas, compliments of Don Shepherd, Demetrius' father.

"I wish we could stay here forever," Angel told her husband as he wrapped his arms around her and pulled her close.

"I can see why. It's beautiful here."

"It's not just the beauty," Angel told him. "It seems so peaceful here. There's nobody pulling on you, expecting things that you shouldn't be doing. And there's nobody pulling on me, expecting me to be something I'm probably never going to be."

Demetrius planted a kiss on his wife's forehead. He knew that she was still upset with her mother for questioning whether or not the two of them belonged together. After their wedding, Angel had pulled him aside and told him that her mother was worried about them, something about the bible saying, 'how can two walk together if they do not agree'. But Demetrius had told her right then and there, that they didn't have a problem, because no two people on the face of the earth could be more suited for each other. He lifted her head to face him as he told her again, "We are perfect for each other, Angel. You don't have to worry about us. If I don't know anything, I know that God sent you to me. We're meant to be."

Smiling she said, "Even though our upbringing was totally different. And the fact that my parents are preachers doesn't bother you anymore."

Demetrius waved the thought off. "That's their life. They can stay in North Carolina, preaching the Gospel and calling down angels on as many people as they want. They have nothing to do with the way we live back in Ohio."

"What about your daddy?" Angel questioned. "I don't like the fact that everything we have comes through him. Why can't you just get a regular job? I know you can't play baseball anymore but you could coach, right?"

He leaned away a bit, still looking into her eyes. "Oh so now that you've got the ring, you all of a sudden have a problem with the way I make a living?"

"It's not that, Demetrius. I know who you are and how good of a heart you have. I just worry that that I might lose you. And I couldn't bare being without you."

Demetrius pulled himself out of the lounge chair, picked Angel up and ran down towards the ocean with her.

"Don't you dare, Demetrius. I don't have on a swim cap and I just got my hair done."

Demetrius wasn't trying to hear it. He threw her in the water and then jumped in behind her. She flapped one arm while trying to wipe the ocean water from her face with the other. When Demetrius reached her, he grabbed hold of the flailing arm. "Calm down woman. I got you."

"You shouldn't have thrown me in here."

"I had to. I need to show you something."

"But you know I can't swim that good."

Demetrius didn't respond. He just wrapped one arm around Angel and stroked the water with the other arm. They rode the wave that came upon them and then drifted all the way back to the beach. Just as Angel began to relax, they slid into the wet sand. Instead of lifting her out of the water, Demetrius put both arms around her and let the back of her head sink into the sand as he kissed her over and over again.

Angel forgot about her hair as she basked in the love that she had found. "I love you, boo."

He kissed her again, then lifted her from the sand. "I love you too. See how I kept you safe in the water?"

Angel nodded.

"So, don't you ever doubt that I'm going to always be right here, by your side, keeping you safe."

"We'll be together forever, even if we have to go back to the real world and deal with our families, right?" Angel looped an arm around Demetrius' arm as they walked back

"Nothing and nobody is going to split us up. They already tried and failed. So, that's the end of their story... but ours is just beginning."

~~~~

Demetrius yawned, stretched and then opened his eyes. His wife was in the bed with him. They had been apart for so long that he'd forgotten how soundly he slept when she was next to him. "What time is it?"

Angel glanced at the clock on her night stand. "Almost nine."

He yawned again. "Why didn't you wake me? I've got some business to take care of today."

"On a Saturday?"

"The work don't stop, Baby. I got to make them dollars." Demetrius then reached out and pulled Angel closer to him. "But I can be persuaded to stay in bed a little longer if you want to work on making our baby."

"I don't know, Demetrius. The kids will be getting up wanting breakfast soon."

"Don't be like that Angel. Them boys know better than to knock on our door if it's locked. Just lay here with me for a little while longer." Demetrius was desperate to see a smile on his wife's face. They had once been so happy. Demetrius had rushed home from work every night just to be with her.

He'd made many mistakes over the last few years and he'd hurt Angel more times than Demetrius ever imagined that he would. His father had been a horrible husband and Demetrius had vowed to be a better man than Don Shepherd. For the first eleven years of their marriage he had kept his vows.

If he had the power to take these last three years back, he would do it in a heartbeat. But looking in Angel's eyes, Demetrius couldn't deny the hurt he still saw there. A strand of her hair swept across her face. Demetrius put it behind her ear and then rested his hand on her face. "You're still the most beautiful woman in the world to me."

Her lip twisted as she glared at him.

"You don't believe me?" Demetrius pulled her tightly into his arm. "Let me show you how beautiful I think you are." As he lowered his head, putting his lips to her there was a knock on the door.

"Mama…Mama."

Angel jumped up and rushed to the door. She opened it and picked Dam up. He was crying, so Angel wiped the tears from his face. "What's wrong, Dam? Were you scared?"

"I didn't know where you were. We're not at home anymore," Dam told her.

Angel put Dam on the bed between her and Demetrius. "We are home baby. This is where we live now."

"But where is granny?"

"We talked about this, Dam. Don't you remember? I told you that we were going to live with daddy from now on."

Dam then turned his precious little face toward Demetrius. He pointed at the man in bed with his mother. "Is this my daddy?"

Demetrius got out of bed and began walking toward the bathroom.

"Where are you going?" Angel asked him.

"I told you that I had to get to work. I'm going to jump in the shower and then head on out."

"Wait a minute, Demetrius. Don't just walk away like this. Can you at least say something to Dam?"

Demetrius turned toward Angel. "Why do you call him Dam? I thought his name was Obadiah or something crazy like that?"

She nodded. It is Obadiah. His middle name is Damerae which means boy of joy. But he has to grow into those names."

"Don't you think it's a little curious that all my other sons first name begins with a D, but you decided to go off the script with this kid?" Demetrius didn't give her a chance to answer the question. He went into the bathroom and shut the door behind him.

Demetrius leaned against the door trying to calm the rage that was boiling in him at the thought of Frankie Day's son being in his house. But he had made a bargain with his wife, and if she could hold up to her end, he would try to at least tolerate the kid.

Thirteen

Angel didn't like the way Dam was being treated. So, she hadn't treated Demetrius all that well in the first week of her homecoming either. Her husband was getting frustrated with the fact that they were only sleeping in the bed together, and doing nothing at all to conceive the little girl he desperately wanted.

Besides ignoring her husband, Angel also got on her knees in prayer every morning and every night. But she wasn't just praying for Dam. She prayed for all her children. DeMarcus was doing great, he was focused on college. Dontae was a normal, shy little kid. But Angel worried that he followed behind Dee too much. And that was the problem, because Dee was changing in ways that Angel hadn't noticed before she'd left for North Carolina; but now that she was back home, she knew for sure that something was up with her son.

"How was your day?" she asked Dee and Dontae as they jumped in the car. She had just picked them up from school, and was on her way to get DeMarcus because Demetrius still wouldn't let their oldest have a car.

"It was fun, Mama. I got first place in the math contest."

"You're just a regular math genius, aren't you?" Angel was so proud of Dontae. He truly applied himself to his school work. He would make something of himself one of these days.

But as she glanced at Dee who had just shoved Dam's hand away from his and then flopped against the backseat and sulked, she asked, "What's wrong with you, Dee? Why are you being so mean to Dam?"

"Why did you have to bring him with you to pick us up? Daddy doesn't want him here and neither do I." Dee scowled at them.

"What a mean thing to say. Why on earth would you think that about your daddy?" Angel hoped and prayed that Demetrius hadn't told his sons how he feels about Dam.

"Don't pay him any attention, Mama," Dontae said. "Dee is just mad because he got detention again today."

"Again?" This was the first Angel was hearing about any detention.

"I am not. I'm mad because Dam took my race car and won't give it back," Dee proclaimed.

But Dontae, wasn't letting his brother off the hook so fast. "Yeah, Mom. This is Dee's third detention this month. The teacher is threatening to suspend him."

For that bit of news, Dee reached over and punched Dontae in the arm. Dontae swung back and Angel had to pull the car over to break the fight up. Then Dee snatched the race car out of Dam's hand.

Dam cried, reaching for the car, he said, "Daddy."

And at that moment, Angel knew that Dam only wanted the car because it had once belonged to Demetrius. Dee had Demetrius' unconditional love, Dam did not, so Angel took the car from Dee and gave it back to Dam.

"It's mine," Dee complained.

"I know it is," she told her son. "But can you please share with your brother. You hardly play with that old car anymore."

Dee wrapped his arms around his chest. "I don't want to share with him... don't even want him here."

Angel was tired of trying to reason with Dee, she pointed in his direction and said, "You're coming to church with me tonight. I think you need a little Jesus right about now."

"Daddy said I don't have to go to no dumb old church." Dee defiantly crossed his arm around his chest.

Angel didn't respond to Dee, she just got back in the car and drove over to the high school to pick up DeMarcus.

But later that night as she was getting dressed for evening service, Demetrius came into her bedroom and asked, "What is this Dee is talking about? He's says you're trying to make him go to church."

Her husband said those words as if she had offered her son a cigarette or was signing him up for a ballet class, when she knew good and well that her son was not about to take such a girly class. "Yes, he should be dressed and waiting for me along with the rest of them."

Demetrius closed the door behind him and walked over to Angel as he said, "No."

"What do you mean, no?" Since Angel had become a Christian she had spent Sunday morning and Wednesday evening in church when she was at her parents' place. But when she was at home, she only went to church on Sundays so she wouldn't have to argue with Demetrius about how often she was away from the house. She also hadn't argued with him about the kids going to church. They normally stayed home with him on Sunday mornings. But she wasn't going to do that anymore. Her children needed Jesus just as much as she needed Him.

"You know exactly what I mean," Demetrius told her. "My sons don't need this crutch you call Jesus. They are well taken care of."

"Oh really, well then why is Dee getting called into detention so much then?"

Demetrius shrugged. "Kids act out. You were in North Carolina taking care of that other kid when you should have been at home with us, and Dee was just showing out. But you're home now, and he'll calm back down."

"He received another detention today, Demetrius. So, exactly how calm do you think he is?" Her hands were on her hips, ready to do battle. Angel hadn't quiet mastered the submit to your husband yet. The way she saw it, Demetrius wasn't submitting to the Lord, so she wasn't all that interested in submitting to him.

"Why don't you try sitting at home with him and maybe playing a board game or watching a movie? The kid misses his mother."

"And his mother is getting ready to take him to church," Angel raised her voice.

"No, you're not."

Angel pointed at the door as she told him, "If you don't go out there and tell that boy to get ready for church, then I am going to have the biggest headache of my life when I get back home. It might just stay with me for a week, or maybe a month."

Glaring at her, Demetrius said, "What difference would a headache make? You haven't let me touch you all week."

"You don't know what I had on my mind for tonight."

"And you call yourself a Christian… in here blackmailing me? How does that jive with your religion, Ms. Holy Roller?"

It didn't, Angel could admit that to herself. But she knew that her husband wanted a little girl, had been wanting her for years, and if she had to use that little girl in order to get her boys to church then she was going to use whatever leverage she had. "Are you going to tell them to get ready so we can go or not?"

"Take Dam with you, and leave my boys out of it. Besides, Dee and Dontae have basketball practice on Wednesday nights."

"When did you sign them up for that?" Angel asked, giving in to the fact that she had just lost this battle.

"Three weeks ago."

"Okay, you take them to basketball. But when basketball camp ends, I'll make sure that none of their activities are on Wednesday night again. Because they will be going to church with me."

"Have you forgotten what I do for a living, Angel? Church is no place for a gangster and his children."

"What you need to do is bring yourself to church and fall down on the altar and beg God to forgive you for the way you've chosen to live your life."

Anger flared in his eyes as he declared, "If I didn't live my life this way, you and the kids wouldn't have life at all. So, is that what you want, Angel? Do you want me to tell the Columbians that I won't be their errand boy anymore, and then just wait here until they come and slit all of our throats?"

"What have you gotten us involved in, Demetrius? How dare you put my kids at risk like this?"

"Get off your high horse, Angel. You enjoy the lifestyle that we have, you just don't want to know where it comes from. So, you can go to your church, praise the Lord and pretend to be so above it all."

"Get out of this room, Demetrius." She pointed toward the door.

He shook his head. "You're not putting me out of my own bed again. You can forget that." He stepped to her, lowered himself so that they were facing each other, nose to nose. "Get with the program, Angel. Or you can get out, and I'll have another woman in here raising my sons."

She could have spat in his face for the way he was talking to her. But instead, she shoved him away and pointed a finger at the door again. "I need to finish getting dressed for church, can you please give me some privacy."

DeMarcus decided to come to church with her and Dam, which made Angel happy that two of her boys were in the house of the Lord. KeKe and her oldest sat with them, while Dam and KeKe's two youngest went to children's church.

Praise and worship was on fire, DeMarcus was enjoying himself. Angel prayed that when Pastor Fisher stood behind the pulpit he would preach something that DeMarcus could take back home to his father, something that would wake Demetrius up. But when Pastor Fisher started preaching the word of God, Angel felt as if she was the one being kicked in the gut.

Pastor Fisher read from Luke chapter 6:30-36

Give to everyone who asks of you. And from him who takes away your goods do not ask them back. And just as you want men to do to you, you also do to them likewise. But if you love those who love you, what credit is that to you? For even sinners love those who love them. And if you do good to those who do good to you, what credit is that to you? For even sinners do the same. And if you lend to those from whom you hope to receive back, what credit is that to you? For even sinners lend to sinners to receive as much back. But love your enemies, do good, and lend, hoping for nothing in return; and your reward will be great, and you will be sons of the Most High. For He is kind to the unthankful and evil. Therefore be merciful, just as your Father also is merciful.

She wanted to shout at Pastor Fisher for stepping all over her toes with his message, but at times it seemed as though Demetrius was her enemy but she hadn't done anything good to or for him during those times. She had been waiting for him to do and be the man she wanted him to be before she would do or be the woman he wanted her to be. God wanted so much more from His Children.

Tears streamed down Angel's face as Pastor Fisher finished his message. She stood and walked down to the altar for prayer, and at that moment, Angel finally felt all the anger she had been carrying against Demetrius subside. She was finally free of it.

As they were driving home that night, DeMarcus asked her, "Are you and Dad getting divorced?"

Angel stopped at the red light and glanced over at her son. "Why would you ask me something like that?"

"You're different around Dad. It doesn't seem like you want to be here anymore. I'm only asking because I'll be leaving for college in a few months, and I'd hate to get a call from you or dad while I'm away telling me that y'all have split up."

Angel hadn't realize that her actions against Demetrius were affecting her children. But with DeMarcus asking her about a divorce and Dee acting out in school, she wondered if things were better at home if DeMarcus would stop worrying about grown folks' business and if Dee would stop acting out. "I'm sorry, DeMarcus. Things have been difficult lately, but I promise you, I'm going to do everything possible, from this moment forward to love your father and to mend this family.

Fourteen

Angel got up bright and early the next morning and fixed breakfast for the family. She made pancakes, cheese eggs, bacon, sausage and hash browns. When she and Demetrius first got together she used to fix this meal for Demetrius all the time. He claimed he loved her pancakes and he acted as if the cinnamon she added to the pancake batter had been some kind of secret ingredient.

"Am I dreaming?" Demetrius asked as he entered the kitchen. "Or am I smelling cinnamon pancakes?"

"I don't think you're dreaming," Angel told him. She turned around from the stove and greeted her husband with a smile on her face. "Have a seat and I'll fix your plate."

"Where are the boys?"

"Upstairs, getting ready for school."

"They already ate?"

"They wolfed that food down like it was their last meal or something. She put his plate in front of him.

Demetrius eyes got big. "You made home fries too?"

Angel nodded. "I made all your favorites this morning. I thought you'd like it. Was I right?"

"You know it." he said; but the look on his faced seemed to speak of mixed blessings. Demetrius hadn't yet picked up his fork, he just kept staring at it.

"What's wrong?"

Clearing his throat, he looked back up at Angel. "I'm just wondering why you're not eating anything."

She laughed at him and then took his plate away. "Here, I'll fix you another one. And I'll eat the one I gave you." Shaking her head as she fixed his second plate, Angel said, "I can't believe you thought that I would poison you."

He accepted the plate from her, waited until she sat down. She prayed over the food. Then he said, "We got into a fight last night, remember?"

"I remember."

"So, you have to admit, it's a little suspect that you all of a sudden want to fix my favorite breakfast foods."

"Nothing suspect about it at all. I just think it's time that I do right by you and our marriage."

Demetrius looked skeptical. "What exactly does that mean, Angel?"

"It means that I'm ready to give us a try again."

Demetrius took her hand in his while his eyes implored her to tell him something good. "Do you think you really can forgive me, and give us a real chance?"

She nodded. "I can. I really think I can."

Demetrius smiled as he took a fork full of his pancakes. He and Angel ate in silence, but all of a sudden, he put his fork down and turned to her. "This isn't some kind of blackmail to get me to spend time with Dam is it?"

She shook her head. "I'm going to pray about your relationship with Dam, but I'm not going to force you to do anything that you don't want to do. I'm tired of fighting with you, so all I ask is that you try not to mistreat Dam, because he doesn't deserve that."

He went back to eating without responding, but there was still a smile on his face, so Angel felt it was time to tell her husband what she planned to do today. "Do you mind dropping the kids off at school this morning?"

"Sure, what do you have planned?"

"I'm taking Dam to visit your father."

Pushing his plate away, Demetrius turned to her with a lifted brow. "Why would you do that?"

"I want Don to know that I'm not angry with him anymore and I want him to see his grandson."

Demetrius' jaw tightened. "I don't think that's a good idea. Don is the reason for all the problems we've had, and if it wasn't for him sending you to…" Demetrius couldn't finish his sentence. He stood up. "I need to get to work. Do whatever you want."

"You could come with us. I'm sure your father would love to see you."

"And have him look at me with pity once he sees in the flesh a child that I'm forced to take care of or lose you… all because of what he did to us. No thank you, I will not visit him with you and Dam." Demetrius' face filled with fury as he glared at his wife for even asking such a thing.

"Why do you hate him so much? What has Dam ever done to you?"

Angel and Demetrius both swung around to see DeMarcus standing there with just as much anger and indignation as his father had.

"Ask your mother," Demetrius threw back at his son.

"I'm asking you." DeMarcus wasn't backing down. "You're the one who treats Dam like he's not a part of this family. I've watched

106

my mother cry too many times to count about the way you treat her and Dam. And I don't get it."

"I don't answer to you. You answer to me, and don't forget it. Now go get your brothers so I can take y'all to school."

"No, I'm not going anywhere with you. Not until you tell me what is going on around here. You wouldn't even let Mom bring Dam home for all these years, and now that he's finally here, you're still acting like his presence offends you, and I want to know why? Tell me why, Dad?"

Angel tried to step between her husband and son. She held onto to DeMarcus' arm and tried to move him out of the kitchen. "Go get your brothers, this is between me and your father."

But DeMarcus wouldn't be moved, he kept his eyes on Demetrius as he demanded, "Answer me."

"He's not my son, okay. Are you happy now that you've got your answer?"

Angel couldn't believe that he said those words to her son. Lord, it seemed like the more she prayed the more things fell apart.

DeMarcus yelled back at Demetrius. "I'm not your son either. So, are you ashamed to be seen with me also? Do you hate me as much as you hate Dam?"

Pain etched across Demetrius' face the moment those words dropped from DeMarcus' mouth. "That's crazy. You are my son and I love you. I love your mom. I love our family, DeMarcus, but this has been hard for me to deal with."

"No, because I think you're lying anyway. Mom says that Dam is your son. And now you want to say that he's not. You're just trying to cover up for all the women you've been with, and don't think I haven't noticed. I'm sick of you and I can't wait to get out of this house for good."

When the day began, Angel thought she had set a clear path. She was working on treating Demetrius the way he deserved to be treated as her husband and she had made arrangements to visit Don Shepherd. But DeMarcus' blow up had changed her outlook. It seemed to Angel that her family kept taking one step forward and then two steps backward. She didn't know if they were too fractured to ever be put back together again, but she wasn't giving up on God. Angel was going to keep praying, keep doing what she knew was right and then patiently wait on God.

Dr. Willie Mitchell, a preacher who had visited her parent's church, had ministered and taught the congregation a simple equation: faith + patience = the promise. So she was just going to keep on believing and fight her way through all the madness with her faith.

After DeMarcus' blow up, Angel had almost stayed home, thinking that she didn't have the energy to drive four hours away to see Don. But if she didn't do it now, she would probably lose her nerve. Angel needed to see Don, because she needed to know if she could ever forgive this man. It was obvious by his actions that Demetrius hadn't forgiven his father yet, so it was up to Angel to bridge the gap.

She and Dam arrived at Elkton Federal Prison and after being cleared for their visit, they sat waiting for Don to enter the visitor's room. Angel was talking to Dam, explaining where they were and who they were waiting to see, when the door opened and Don entered the room. He wore a light blue prison shirt and navy blue pants, with a pair of black work shoes. The entire outfit couldn't have cost more than a hundred dollars. But Don looked debonair in it just as if he was sporting one of his thousand dollar suits.

Angel smiled and then pointed towards Don as he walked their way. "Your papa is here."

"Where?" Dam asked as he stood up, searching the room.

"I'm right here," Don told him as he lifted Dam up, swung him around and hugged him tightly.

When he put Dam down, Dam had this strange expression on his face. He touched Don's arm and then asked, "Are you really my papa?"

"I sure am." Don was beaming at the sight of him.

But then Dam said, "Why does someone want to kill you?"

Don turned to Angel. "What did he say?"

Angel put Dam in her lap and asked, "What did you say to Papa?" She thought she'd heard him correctly, but she didn't want to deliver that news without being sure of what she heard.

"Someone wants to kill Papa?" Dam repeated.

Don flopped down in the chair next to Angel. He stared at Dam for a long moment. "How does he know that?"

"Just because he said it, doesn't mean he's right. But Dam is very special. He will one day be used mightily by God and he sees things that others don't see."

"Like an attack on my life?" Don kept staring at Dam, then he said, "Tell you what, lil' man. If someone does kill me in here, I'll die a happy man because I had a chance to see you." He looked back up at Angel and said, "He looks just like Demetrius at that age."

"I wish you had some pictures so I could show Demetrius, because he sure doesn't believe it." Angel then waved her comment away. "But we didn't come here to talk about that. I know that family is important to you, so I wanted to introduce you to your grandson."

"You're a good woman, Angel. I didn't think you were right for my son when the two of you first got together. But you've been down for this family and I thank you for that."

It was strange, but Angel didn't resent Don's comment. She and Demetrius were like oil and water these days. Because as she sought more and more of God's light, Demetrius seemed to be sinking further into darkness.

Don took Dam in his arm and the two talked for a half an hour. They were so comfortable with each other, you'd of thought Don had been around him the entire time. Dam leaned over and kissed his papa on the cheek and then he whispered something in his ear.

Angel then heard Don say, "Sure, you can pray for me, what could it hurt?"

Dam held out both his hands. Don took one of them and Angel took the other, just as he had seen done countless times at her parents' church. And as her son started to pray and call down the power of God and His angels to protect Don from men that would do him harm, Angel realized something else… her mother had been right. Dam was supposed to stay with them and learn about the power of God which her father taught every Sunday. Their ministry was about making disciples of God, and Martin and Maxine Barnes sure made a disciple out of her son.

"Amen, in Jesus name I pray," Dam said as he finished his prayer. He then told his Papa, "You'll be alright now, Papa. I will see you again."

Don glanced over at Angel, then he looked back at Dam and said, "Good. That's real good."

When they left the prison and were driving back home, Dam was seated in the back playing with his race care. He put it the car down as he told her, "I'm going to pray that Papa gives his life to God."

Smiling at her little blessing from God as she drove up the highway, she said, "I'm sure Papa will one day thank you for that." Then she asked, "Have you prayed the same for your dad?" Hoping that maybe Dam could do something about the unequally yoked situation she was dealing with on the daily.

"No," Dam said simply, "God doesn't think Daddy is ready yet."

"Oh, okay." Dam's words made her wonder if she was wasting her time, praying for Demetrius right now. But then Angel shook her head and almost laughed out loud. She was listening to a three year old as if he was some grown man already leading a ministry and setting the world on fire.

When they arrived at home later that night, Angel discovered that Demetrius had picked the kids up, ordered pizza and taken DeMarcus on a test drive. "You've been busy," Angel said as she sat Dam at the table and fed him the peanut butter and jelly sandwich he'd been repeatedly asking for during the last hour of their drive home.

"Yeah, the boys are fed, so you don't have to fix them anything. I sent them upstairs to get in the tub."

"And what of this test drive, DeMarcus told me about before I could even step a foot into the house?"

Demetrius sat down at the kitchen island, put a hand under his chin. "I caved. I felt so bad about telling DeMarcus about Dam this morning that I promised to buy him a car."

"What kind of car did he talk you into?" Angel asked good naturedly.

"I had him test drive a Bonneville, but DeMarcus wasn't feeling it. So, we're going to look at a Mustang tomorrow."

"Pushover." Angel laughed at him as she handed Dam his sandwich. After Dam ate his sandwich, Angel took him upstairs, gave him a bath, put his night clothes on and then she laid her very sleepy child in his bed. She kissed his forehead and then headed to her own bedroom.

Angel was so tired from the drive to and from Elkton Federal prison that she wanted to fall in bed and sleep for two days. But as she opened her bedroom door, the smell of vanilla scented candles greeted her. The lights were out, but she could see from the glow of the candles that the bathroom door was open.

She closed the bedroom door behind her as she took baby steps toward the bathroom. Demetrius was standing there, holding a red rose in his hand. She glanced over at the tub and noted the rose pedals atop bubble filled water. "You ran a bath for me?" He hadn't done that in years.

Demetrius nodded as he held out the roses for Angel to take them. "I don't want to fight anymore."

"Me either." She took the roses, inhaled the scent and then laid them on the sink. "That bath looks very inviting. I just hope I don't fall asleep in it."

"If you're worried about falling asleep, I could get in there with you," Demetrius offered. His brow lifted as he waited on her response.

"Sounds good to me," Angel said as she started unbuttoning Demetrius' shirt.

Fifteen

Demetrius was feeling like the man again. He and Angel had spent a blissful weekend together, making love and making plans for the future. Most of Angel's plans included Dam. And even though Demetrius wasn't totally on board, he decided that having his wife happy was worth the sacrifice. So, he kept his mouth shut and just nodded as she spoke of Dam and all his exploits.

Demetrius doubted that he would ever grow to love Dam, because every time he looked at the kid, he imagined Frankie putting his hands on his woman. But his opposition to the kid was tearing his family apart, so Demetrius had come to terms with the fact that he didn't want to lose his family. And he certainly didn't want his own children turning on him as DeMarcus had done.

During breakfast Demetrius sat at the table with all of the children, ate the food that Angel cooked for them. He laughed and chatted with his children and was thankful that Dam hadn't said a word to him.

But as Demetrius drove to work, he realized something that puzzled him. The kid never said anything to him. Sometimes, Demetrius caught Dam staring as if he was trying to figure him out. But not once did he open his mouth, not even to say good morning. Angel thought her kid was so perfect, but he didn't even have enough manners to speak to the man who was putting food in his belly and clothes on his back. He was going to say something to Angel about that.

Al pulled up at the office at the same time Demetrius did. He rushed Demetrius into the office and said, "We've got a situation."

"Who did what to who now?" The street life wasn't no joke… these boys go hard and then a lot of them end up dead.

"Somebody tried to shank your father last night.."

"What? Is he okay?" His dad couldn't die in prison, because if that happened, he'd be stuck leading this family business for the rest of his life.

"He's good. The guards handled the situation." Al slid his finger across his throat.

"So now the guards are up in there killing folks?" Demetrius didn't want no parts of prison. They were worse than these hustlers on the street.

"Would you have rather that they just sent the little imp back to his cell so he could get at Don another night?"

"I don't get it. Don't we pay those guards to watch out for Dad? So, what happened? How did anyone even get close enough to make an attempt on his life?"

"The way I got it, the guy was let into Don's cell during the shift change. Don was taking care of business when one of our guards checked on him. He hauled the dude back to his cell, finished the job and then sounded the alarm."

Demetrius sat down and pondered this news. When he looked back at Al, he said, "So, we need to figure out which guard opened dad's cell. Because this can't happen again."

"Already on it. Don pretended to be sleep, but he watched the guard open his cell. So, I'm sending some of my boys to pay him a visit tonight."

"Good. But try to find out why this dude wanted dad dead. We need to know if anyone else is coming after him. I mean, it couldn't be the Columbians could it… I'm doing everything they wanted, right?"

Al left the office and Demetrius, leaned back in his seat and exhaled. His dad almost died last night. He hadn't visited the man in over a year, and had ignored Angel when she'd asked him to drive up there with her. Demetrius wanted desperately to get over the issues he had with his father, but the truth of the matter was, when he looked at Dam, he didn't just think about what Frankie did to Angel… he also remembered that all of it was his father's fault.

~~~~

The kids were at school and Angel and Dam were running around the house playing hide and go seek when the phone rang. It was Don, calling collect. Angel thought the call was for Demetrius, but once she accepted the call, Angel discovered that Don was calling for her.

"He was right," Don said in a whispered tone.

"Who was right?"

"Dam. He said someone was trying to kill me and they came after me last night. And I didn't even have to kill 'em. The guards took care of business for me."

"Are you telling me that this other man is dead?"

"I'm telling you that I'm alive and if it hadn't been for Dam I'd be dead right now. If he hadn't of prayed for me like that, I wouldn't have been on the lookout, and I would have missed this plot against me."

"Praise God. I'm so glad you are still alive, Don. My sons need both of their grandfathers." Angel walked over to the mirror and looked at her reflection. She was saying words about Don that she never thought she would ever say… and the strangest thing of all, was that she truly meant it. She had once thought of Don Shepherd as nothing more than a monster, but her wounds had been healed by the power of God, and now she could even have compassion for a man like him. Because she had forgiven him.

"Look Angel, I wanted to talk to you about Demetrius and Dam."

Angel shook her head as if Don was sitting in her living room. "Demetrius doesn't have anything to do with Dam. He's trying to tolerate Dam, but that's it."

"Why don't you get him to take a DNA test? That way he'll know without a doubt that Dam is his."

She couldn't bring herself to confess about how she had bungled the home DNA test that she tried to do. By the time the swabs were sent to the DNA testing facility, they weren't able to do the test because of contamination and evidently that quick swab of Demetrius' jaw wasn't enough.

So, she told him, "He has refused to do the test. I've asked, but I think for Demetrius it would be worse if he had a piece of paper that told him Dam wasn't his."

"If he won't do it. Then get an attorney and send paperwork to the prison so that I can take the test. That way you can get the paternity match based on me, then Demetrius will have to accept it."

Tears blurred, Angel's eyes. She thought God had let her down the night she'd tried to get Demetrius' DNA and had failed, but all the while, God had another way planned. "You would do that for us?"

"Send the paperwork."

~~~~

Two things happened the day Dam turned four. Demetrius actually showed up to Dam's birthday party. The family stood around as Dam blew out the candles. Everything was going great. A clown and a magician had shown up to entertain the kids and Dam was having a ball. But then Angel all of a sudden felt ill. She ran to the bathroom and threw up every bit of the scrumptious chocolate cake she'd just eaten.

Demetrius came into the bathroom behind her, just as he had the last time she'd ran into the bathroom to throw up. "Are you okay," he asked.

"I don't know what happened. I was feeling fine, and then I felt nauseous."

"Is this the first time you've thrown up?"

"Yes, but I've been feeling nauseous all week, and then the feeling would just go away." She stood at the sink and brushed her teeth. She hadn't thought much of it, but the look on Demetrius' face as she glanced at him through the mirror, caused her to put the tooth brush down and turn around to face him. "You don't think?"

He nodded. "I do. I'm going to run to the drugstore to get the pregnancy test. Is that alright with you?"

"Yes, my love. Go get it." Angel sat down on her bed as she waited for her husband to come back with the test. They had come a long way in the last few months. Her husband was once again the man she had fallen in love with fifteen years ago.

Angel could hardly believe the way they were now treating one another. But then again she did believe it, because she believed in the power of prayer. That same power would one day help Demetrius to love Dam as much as he loved his other children. But for now, his presence was enough. Dam had even noticed the change in his father. He now greeted him in the mornings with a simple hello.

That was the extent of Dam's and Demetrius' relationship, but Angel wasn't giving up hope… not yet… not until there was no breath left in her body to seek God in prayer.

~~~~

She was pregnant.

"Baby, do you know what this means?" Demetrius picked her up and swung her around.

"Yeah, it means that you better not stress me out like you did while I was carrying Dam."

Demetrius gently sat Angel down on their bed. Then he sat down next to her, and put her hand in his. "I know I will never be able to make these last few years up to you. I have done you so wrong, for something that wasn't your fault. I want you to know how truly sorry I am for what I did to you. I'm just thankful that you forgave me and decided to keep our family together."

Tears burned her eyes as she listened to her husband express everything that was on his heart. She gently touched his face and placed her lips on his. As she leaned away, she said, "I have worked very hard at forgiving you, Demetrius. I know the kind of man you are down deep and I'm praying that the Demetrius I fell in love with will rise up in you again."

"Would that be enough for you, Angel?"

She took a moment to think over his question before answering, then shook her head. "It would be a good start, but it's not enough."

Demetrius stood and walked over to the window. His hands were stuffed into his pockets as he looked out at their land. "I know what you want from me, Angel. When we first got married you promised that you would never turn into some religious nut."

"Demetrius…" she began.

He held up a hand. "Hear me out. Because you're not some religious nut running around here trying to convert everybody. But I can see that it is important to you that the boys share your faith, so I'm going to stop fighting you about taking them to church. But Angel, I need you to understand that I'm never going to be interested in anything to do with God."

She walked up behind him, put her hand on his arm. "Why won't you at least come to church with me, Demetrius? Just give God a chance."

"I can't."

"Will you at least tell me why? I promise I won't badger you about this, but I need to know why you won't even give God a chance."

"It's not me." He swung around to face her. At that moment she saw regret and sorrow in his eyes. "Don't you get it, Angel? I've done too much. Your God would never want a man like me."

"If I still want a man like you, what makes you think that God doesn't?"

Demetrius had no answer for her. He shrugged as he put a hand on her belly and then in a sing-songy way, he said, "You're having my baby… having my little girl."

"Don't go counting on some little girl before I give birth," she said, letting him change the subject. Just as Dam had told her last year, Demetrius wasn't ready yet. "And I don't want you pouting in the labor and delivery room if this baby turns out to be a boy."

Demetrius wrapped his arms around his wife. "I promise you this, Angel. I'm going to love this child no matter what it turns out to be. How could I not be happy with something that comes from you and me?"

Angel had been asking herself the same thing since the day Dam was born.

Sixteen

Eight Months Later...

Demetrius and Mo narrowly escaped the ambush that Alejandro set up for them. Sammy had not been so lucky. Three shots to the back had ended Sammy's life. With his Glock in his hand, Demetrius stormed through his office door. Al was waiting on him and Mo.

"This stuff is real y'all. I just found out that Alejandro was the one who put the hit out on Don," Al told them.

"What is this dude's problem?" Demetrius stalked around the room like a lion looking for his prey.

"You know what's wrong with him," Mo said, not taking Demetrius' question well. "We done lost Sammy and several other soldiers all because you slept with that man's woman. I told you that Alejandro wasn't taking that like some sucka."

"And I told you to take him out. But you thought that if I left Tricia alone that would be the end of it. But Alejandro won't quit." Demetrius pointed toward Al. "You heard what Al just said, he tried to take my daddy out over some chick."

"What would you have do if some dude messed with Angel?" Mo challenged, then hung his head as he realized he'd said too much. "I'm sorry man. I know you're still dealing with your own issues. And it's not your fault that Alejandro can't get over the fact that Tricia stepped out on him."

"You don't need to be sorry, I messed up too. But I'm going to fix this problem myself." Demetrius headed for the door. But Al pulled him back.

"Hold on there. I can't let you do this. Not with that wife of yours about to give birth. Don would never forgive me."

"I'm the head of this family now, Al. I'm not some dumb kid that you can push around anymore."

Al shook his head. "Not trying to push you around. But where you are the boss, I'm the enforcer of this family and my job is to keep you from getting dead."

"Well, what you want me to do, Al? Just sit here and wait for this dude to kill us all."

"Go home, Demetrius. Sit with that pretty wife and wait on that baby to come. Then I want you to take that baby to see your daddy."

"And what about Alejandro?" Demetrius looked from Al to Mo.

Mo said, "It wasn't only you who messed up, Demetrius. I misjudged Alejandro because I was benefiting from the business he was bringing us. And I was ticked at you for messing that up."

"So, I'm going to take care of the problem for both of you… got me." Al gave Demetrius and Mo a look that assured them the deed would be done.

Demetrius turned to Mo. "I need you to take money to Sammy's mother. Let her know we will take care of the funeral and that if she needs anything… that's what family is for."

"I'm on it." Mo headed out the door.

Demetrius then turned to Al. Half smiling, half smirking. "You act like you can't stand working with me. But I guess you're still my Uncle Al, huh?"

Al palmed Demetrius' head. "I'm gon' always be your Uncle Al. Now get out of here and go spend time with your family."

In truth, Demetrius was thankful that he was driving home right now, rather than being stretched out, dead as Alejandro wanted him to be. He was angry at the situation and because Sammy was dead. But deep down Demetrius knew that he alone was to blame for what was happening to the family.

He knew the kind of pain Alejandro was dealing with. Angel hadn't even stepped out on him, and he still hadn't been able to forget. But he was at least giving it a try these days. When he arrived home, he made sandwiches for the kids and then rubbed Angel's feet which had swollen so bad that it made it hard to stand for long periods of time.

He'd even moved her to the downstairs bedroom that was right next to the kitchen so she wouldn't have to go up and down those stairs. Angel had resisted the idea of switching bedrooms at first. But Demetrius knew that her hesitation had more to do with the fact that Serena had stayed in that room while Angel had been with her parents, and Demetrius needed someone to help him with the kids.

So he made sure the housekeeper, who cleaned weekly, thoroughly scrubbed that room. Then Demetrius had the room painted the same sage green as their bedroom. He also threw the bed out and had a new one delivered. Angel had forgiven him for his indiscretion with Serena, he knew that based on the way she was now treating him. But that didn't mean she wanted to sleep in a room that resembled the place where her husband laid with another woman.

"Does that feel better?" Demetrius asked as he finished rubbing her feet.

"No," Angel answered honestly. "But thank you for trying."

He gave her a weak smile. "I feel terrible that you've had such horrible pregnancies."

"I know, I know… you wish you could trade places with me."

Demetrius laughed at that. "Are you crazy woman? What man in his right mind would trade places with you right now? I feel for you, but I don't want the problems you've got."

Angel pulled the pillow from behind her back and threw it at her husband. "You just better hope this baby is a girl, because this is baby number five and I'm closing up shop. I want them to take my ovaries when they pull this baby out."

"You better hope your God is listening, because if you give me another rock head boy, then I at least get one more baby."

Just then Dontae, Dee and Dam ran into the room, the three of them shouting at the top of their lungs, "I had it first," "No, I had it first." "Give it back."

Dee was holding the basketball and race car out of their reach. But all of a sudden, Dontae jumped like he was Michael Jordan in Space Jam. He knocked the ball and race car out of Dee's hand. The ball went sailing into the wall, knocking down Angel's beautiful picture of a lady laying in the grass reading a book. The glass frame shattered on the floor. Dam quickly bent down, picked up the race car and ran out of the room.

Demetrius ordered the boys back upstairs and then started cleaning up the mess.

Angel then told him, "I think you're the one who needs to pray that God gives us a girl, because I'm telling you Demetrius Shepherd, I am tired. Five is enough. These boys have been trying my patience for weeks."

"I've tried to keep them out of your hair at night, but I think they miss being around you."

"I think it might be the hormones, but I really need a break. Can you take the boys for a few hours tomorrow and give me some alone time?"

He didn't want to leave his wife when they were dealing with Alejandro. So he said, "I don't think this is a good time. You could have our baby girl any day now."

"I'm not due for another two weeks, Demetrius. But I truly need to rest my mind now."

"You went into labor early with Dam," Demetrius reminded her.

"Dam was a different situation. That boy couldn't wait to get out into this cruel world. But other than my swollen feet, this baby has been no drama at all, and I'm loving it."

"I just don't think that this is a good time to leave you alone."

But Angel said, "I'm going to lose my mind if you don't take your kids and get out of here... all I'm asking for is a few hours. That's it."

Demetrius had increased security around the house. So, even if he and the kids left for a while, there would still be someone there to watch over her. "Tell you what, Dontae and Dee have been asking me to take them fishing for months now. So, if you promise not to leave the house while I'm gone, I'll spend a few hours at the lake with them tomorrow, and then I'll take them out to lunch. Will that be enough time for you?"

"Perfect." She agreed. "But what about Dam?"

"I can't take him with me," Demetrius said, but when he saw the look on his wife's face he added, "Not because I don't want to be bothered. Dam wanders around too much. I don't want to be pulling him out of the lake."

She nodded. "You are right about that. Okay, can you drop him off at the day camp?"

"Man, you don't want to see none of us, do you?"

"That's not true. I am very excited about seeing DeMarcus tomorrow. But he hasn't been here running around the house, breaking things, and dirtying up every section of the house."

"I know, I know. DeMarcus is perfect and our other boys are monsters." Demetrius joked. Then he pointed at her belly, "That's why we need my daughter to hurry up and get here. Maybe she'll calm them down."

~~~~

Angel walked like a turtle and could barely get up and down the stairs in her home. She had resisted Demetrius when he first suggested that she move into the bedroom downstairs, but now as her feet continued to swell and her belly just kept growing, she was thankful that her husband had such a brilliant idea. She was also thankful for the peace and quiet in her house this morning.

Demetrius had made her a cup of tea and brought her a warm wheat donut bright and early this morning, just before leaving the house with the kids. Her husband had finally become the man she had married again. He was thoughtful, loving and always seeking out ways to make her happy. And she had fallen in love with him all over again. No, their marriage wasn't a fairytale, because he still hadn't accepted God into his life… but yet and still things were good between them.

Her marriage had been saved by the one simple thing that Demetrius probably didn't even realize he was doing, but Angel did and it made all the difference. Because these days, Demetrius wasn't just calling Dam 'the kid' or 'that kid'. He was saying Dam's name; and each time he did, it brought a smile to Angel's face.

She opened her bedroom door and slowly made her way to the kitchen. DeMarcus was coming home and she wanted to make him a blueberry crumb cake. She wanted to get it done now because she had the house to herself, and she planned to spend the day listening to music, praying and sleeping.

The house was so quiet that Angel could hear her feet sliding across the floor. When the boys were home she couldn't hear that because of all the running, jumping and yelling. Demetrius loved to tell her that boys would be boys, but Angel just wished that boys could take it down a notch.

As she passed the kitchen counter, she noticed Dam's back pack on one of the counter chairs. She opened the bag and just as she thought, his lunch was in there. If she took the back pack to the day camp, that would cut into her down time, she really didn't want to do that. But Dam would need something to eat. So, she picked up the phone and called the camp.

"Hello, my name is Angel Shepherd. My husband dropped our son there this morning."

"Yes, Mrs. Shepherd, how are you this morning?" the camp secretary asked.

"I'm doing good. But Dam left his lunch and I was wondering if you all had something he could eat, or if I need to bring his back pack?"

"Oh, don't go to any trouble. We fix sandwiches here everyday for children who don't have anything to eat. We'll just give Dam one of those."

"Thank you so much," Angel said, grateful for the fact that she didn't have to leave the house, because that was the last thing she wanted to do.

She wanted peace and quiet, but now that she was in the house alone, she admitted that the place was just too quiet. Her boys brought life to this big house. But as Angel maneuvered around the kitchen mixing her crumb cake and putting it in the oven without some little munchkins following her around, begging to lick the bowl or the spoon, she appreciated her husband so much at that moment.

Angel put the cake in the oven and then went back to her room and turned on her CD player to lay down and listen to John P. Kee.. God had been good to her and her family. Everything wasn't the way it should be yet, because she still had so many issues with Demetrius. But he'd come a long way from the man who almost threw his family away. During their worst moments, Angel had come to realize that love alone would never be enough.

What kept her in this fight was her belief that God would one day take hold of Demetrius and cause him to walk up right before the Lord. Her husband would let go of the street life and embrace a new life in Christ. Angel couldn't wait to see how sweet life would be with her husband once they were on one accord. Both serving the Lord and teaching their children to do the same.

Angel drifted off to sleep dreaming about this new life in Christ that her entire family would one day experience. She was so caught up in her hopes and dreams for her family, that she didn't wake up until the smell of her cake burning drifted into her bedroom.

Angel jumped up a bit too quick. She felt something hot and sticky trickle down her leg. Her eyes widened as she pulled up her gown, checking to make sure she wasn't bleeding. No blood, but she was standing in a pool of water.

"Oh my God!" Angel couldn't believe this was happening. She'd practically shoved Demetrius and the kids out of the house, because she thought she had at least another week. But a contraction hit, and doubled her over. She panted for breath. When the pain subsided

Angel made her way to the kitchen and turned off the oven. She then picked up the phone and called Demetrius.

He answered on the second ring and said, "Are you enjoying your day?"

Another contraction hit her, she yelled and not until it subsided, was she able to say, "My water broke. I need to get to the hospital."

"What? But I'm an hour away."

"I can call a cab. But can you call Todd at the security booth to make sure he let's the cabbie in to get me."

"I'll do one better than that. I'll have Todd run you to the hospital and I'll meet up with you as soon as I can get there."

Angel went back to the bedroom and grabbed the bag that she packed a month ago for the hospital. She then called her mother. "It's time. I'm on my way to the hospital."

Maxine didn't even think about it. She said, "Your father and I will be there in a few hours. We just need to get on the plane. I packed our suitcases last week for this trip."

Angel was glad to hear it. No matter how old she got or how many babies she had, she still needed her mama. She opened the front door and looked out for Todd. Just as she was looking out the door, Todd was pulling up to the house with another car following behind with two other guys in it.

"Come on Mrs. Angel, I'm going to get you to the hospital," he told her.

"Who are they?" Angel pointed to the car that had pulled up behind Todd.

"Just some extra security personnel that Demetrius hired. Todd threw her bag in the back seat and then helped her into the car.

As he drove off, Angel looked back and sure enough the other two men were following them. She wasn't the first lady of the

United States. She didn't need a security detail. What was Demetrius thinking?

Another contraction hit and Angel turned her thoughts away from Demetrius' paranoia to the pain that was ripping her body apart. "Hurry Todd. I don't want to have this baby in your car."

"No, we don't want that," Todd said as he did sixty miles per hour down a thirty-five mile per hour street.

His speed didn't bother Angel. All she cared about was getting to the hospital before her baby became too distressed. As they pulled into the hospital parking lot, Angel started panting as another contraction took her by storm.

Todd jumped out of the car and got a wheel chair. He put Angel in the chair and pushed her to the nurse station.

Three big burly men stood behind Angel as she provided the intake nurse with the information needed to admit her. She then turned to Todd and said, "You all can leave now. Demetrius should be here shortly."

The two men whom Angel had never been introduced to shook their heads as Todd told her. "We can't leave you, Mrs. Angel. Demetrius has asked us to stick with you until he gets here."

What was going on? Angel wanted to ask, but she knew she wouldn't get the truth out of any of them. But her husband, he had some explaining to do.

Seventeen

As Demetrius sped down the highway, he placed a call to DeMarcus. When DeMarcus picked up he asked, "How far from home are you?"

"I should be there in about twenty minutes."

"Great. Can you pick Dam up from his day camp and meet us at the hospital?"

"At the hospital? Don't tell me mom went into labor already."

"You guessed it. I'm on the highway heading back with Dontae and Dee, so it would really help me out if you could pick your brother up."

"You got it, Dad."

He hung up with DeMarcus and kept pushing it. Dontae yelled from the backseat, "You're going to get a ticket, Dad."

"I better not. I don't have time for a ticket today."

"Can I show Mom the fish I caught?" Dee asked.

"You won't be able to bring your fish into the hospital. You can tell her about it, though."

"I'm going to tell her that my fish was this big." Dee stretched his hands out, much wider than any fish could ever be."

"And I'm going to tell her that you're a big fat liar," Dontae told his brother.

"You do it, hear; and I'll get you," Dee warned.

All he could think about was that his wife was in labor and that his little girl was about to be born. And although he loved his sons more than life itself, Demetrius couldn't take another thirty minutes of their bickering. "Okay, time for the quiet game. The winner will get a dollar and the loser will get introduced to my belt... now say something else." he dared them.

~~~~

DeMarcus pulled up to the day camp. He signed in at the office and then went to Dam's room to pick him up. He was glad that his dad asked him to pick Dam up. Because even though he loved his other brothers, he felt a certain kinship with Dam that he didn't understand. The boy was special to him. And he'd felt this way even before his dad claimed that Dam wasn't his kid.

His parents still had not explained that comment to him. All he'd received was a car and an apology. But that wasn't good enough. One day, DeMarcus was going to make them explain why the two of them sent this family through so much drama.

He opened the door to Dam's room and Dam leaped out of his seat and ran to him. "DeMarcus, you're home!"

DeMarcus bent down and lifted Dam into his arms. "Yes, little man, I'm home. I came to pick you up."

"Yay! I want to go home. I left my toy."

"We'll have to get your toy later, little man. Mom's in the hospital." They walked to the car. DeMarcus buckled Dam in. Then he got behind the wheel getting ready to take off.

Dam unbuckled himself and started jumping around the car. "Want my toy... want my toy."

"Boy, what is wrong with you? Mama is getting ready to have a baby, and you're acting like a baby."

DeMarcus buckled him back in, but Dam unbuckled himself again. "Want my toy! Want my toy!"

"Where is your toy?"

"At home… want my toy… want my toy."

Dad told him to go straight to the hospital, but with the way Dam was acting, he didn't think he'd be able to keep the kid buckled in long enough to get to the hospital. "Okay Dam, you win. If you stay buckled in your seat, I will go back to the house to get your toy. Okay?"

"Yay!" Dam lifted his arms in celebration.

DeMarcus buckled Dam back in and then pulled off, shaking his head. He had never seen Dam act so bratty. Dee and Dontae must be rubbing off on him. Looking through the rearview mirror, DeMarcus told Dam, "You keep acting like this, and I'm going to demote you from being my favorite brother."

Dam laughed as if he was just enjoying his day and had done nothing wrong.

When DeMarcus pulled up to the house, he thought it strange that no one was at the gate. But then he reminded himself that his dad hadn't been home when his mom went into labor. So, the guard probably took her to the hospital. He used his card key to open the gate and drove up to the house.

DeMarcus didn't notice the car that pulled up to the gate, blocking it from closing. Then three men jumped out of the car and walked the distance to the house.

"Okay Dam, let's hurry up. Get your toy so we can go to the hospital and check on Mama." DeMarcus opened the door and Dam ran into the kitchen. He grabbed his back pack off the kitchen counter and ran back towards the front door.

DeMarcus heard a scuffle behind him. He turned and saw three men with guns pointed at him.

~~~~

Demetrius arrived at the hospital. He told Todd that he and one of the guards could go back to the house. But the other guard remained at the hospital in case something broke out while Demetrius was with his family. He went into the labor and delivery room with Angel.

"You made it," she said as her boys ran to the bed and hugged her.

"Don't be sick like last time, Mama. Okay?" Dontae practically pleaded with her.

"I won't be. Don't worry. I'm going to deliver this baby and then go home just like I did when I had you." She kissed Dontae on the top of his head. And then did the same with Dee. "And you."

"So, you're doing okay?" Demetrius had fear in his eyes as he asked the question. He'd witnessed his wife go through a horrible child birth, and he didn't want to see a repeat of that today.

"Stop worrying, Demetrius. You wanted this baby, and he or she is on the way. I'm doing fine." She sucked in a deep breath.

"Have they given you any pain meds yet?" He rushed to her side.

"They're getting ready to," she answered. Then she had a question of her own. "Where's Dam?"

A puzzled look crossed Demetrius' face. "I'm surprised they're not here yet. I asked DeMarcus to pick him up and for them to meet us here. Let me make sure DeMarcus didn't get caught in traffic." He took out his cell phone and called their oldest. His cell rang several times and then went to voicemail. "Hey, where are you? Give me a call when you get this message."

"I'll check with the day camp. See if DeMarcus has picked him up already," Demetrius offered.

But Angel shook her head. "They'll be here in a minute. I wouldn't call them again, or they might think we don't know what's going on."

"I don't know why they would think something like that."

"You left Dam's back pack. So, I had to call them this morning to ask about a lunch for Dam."

Demetrius laughed. "Believe me, Dam let me know that I left his back pack. Evidently his favorite toy was in it. He wanted me to go back home and get it, but I knew you didn't want to see us. So, I told him he'd have to get along without it. But I forgot that the lunch was in there."

"I don't know what's so special about that toy? He acts like it's gold or something," Dee complained.

Angel told him, "When I get out of the hospital I'll show you what's so special about his toys."

~~~~

DeMarcus lifted his hands. "I only have about a hundred dollars on me. But just take it and go."

"No thanks," one of the men said, as he walked up on DeMarcus and hit him hard with the butt of his gun. DeMarcus dropped to the floor.

Dam screamed as he ran towards DeMarcus. "No! Leave my brother alone."

One of the men grabbed Dam as he tried to dive on DeMarcus. Dam struggled with them, trying to break free. "Stop struggling, or I'm going to shoot you."

"Leave us alone," Dam yelled at the men.

The men weren't listening to Dam. One of them asked the leader as he pointed toward DeMarcus, "What do you want us to do with him?"

The leader sized DeMarcus up. "He's too big. I don't want to end up in a fight with him. Just shoot him so he can't follow after us."

The leader then tried to leave the house with Dam. But Dam broke free, and charged the man who held his gun over DeMarcus. The gun went off as the man fell to the ground. DeMarcus was hit.

The leader then grabbed Dam and roughly threw him out of the house. "See you didn't change anything. He's been shot and now we can go."

Eighteen

When Todd arrived at the house he noticed that the gate wasn't closing properly. The other guard took his place behind the security booth as Todd headed down to the house to check things out.

DeMarcus' car was in front of the house. That didn't seem strange because DeMarcus often parked there when he was home. Todd almost turned and went back to the security booth, but then he noticed that the front door was wide open. He stood there for a moment, waiting to see if DeMarcus was going to be rushing out the door. But when there was no movement. He radioed to the security booth. "I'm going in the house. If I don't come back to the booth within two minutes, come check on me."

"Gotcha."

Todd cautiously made his way to the door. Demetrius had been on high alert the last few weeks. No one knew the full extent of what was going on, but Todd knew that some of Demetrius' men had been killed. "DeMarcus?" he called out as he reached the door. "Are you in there?"

At first, Todd didn't hear anything. But as he took a step closer, he could hear someone moaning as if they were in agonizing pain. Todd pulled out his gun and rushed into the house. That's when he saw DeMarcus laying on the floor in a pool of blood.

DeMarcus was alive, but he had lost a lot of blood, so Todd's first call was for an ambulance. He then went to the kitchen, grabbed pot holders and kitchen towels and ran to where DeMarcus was. He dropped down on the floor next to him and found the wound. DeMarcus had been shot right above his hip. Todd applied pressure and then called the security gate.

"Ambulance is on the way, let them in." he hung up and punched in his boss' number with his free hand. Turned the speaker phone on and waited while it rang.

DeMarcus moaned again and lifted his head as Demetrius answered the phone.

"I've got bad news boss."

~~~~

Demetrius was walking back from the cafeteria when his cell rang. He saw that it was Todd so he quickly answered. He stopped in his tracks the moment Todd started talking about bad news.

"Hit me with it. What's going on?"

"I'm at your house. DeMarcus is laying on the floor with a bullet wound. But he's not dead," he quickly added.

"Is he conscious? Can he talk to me?"

"He's kind of going in and out. I don't know how long he's been laying here. But he would have bled out if I hadn't come down to the house."

"Where's Dam?" Demetrius' voiced raised as his hand went to his head and he turned around in circles. Trying to figure out what he needed to do.

"Dam! Dam!" Todd yelled a few times. Then he told Demetrius. "I don't see him. I can't move away from DeMarcus until the ambulance gets here because I'm holding some towels against his wound."

DeMarcus tried to sit up, but Todd pushed him back down. "Lay here until the paramedics get here."

DeMarcus laid back down but he yelled out. "They took Dam. You've got to get him back, Dad."

"Did you hear that?" Todd asked his boss.

"I heard him." Demetrius didn't need to ask who did it… he already knew.

"The paramedics are here. I'll get him to the hospital and you'll be able to talk to him there, okay?"

But DeMarcus yelled, "Tell Mama to pray."

"What did he say?" Demetrius asked Todd.

"He wants you to tell Angel to pray.'

Demetrius didn't respond to that. He said, "Just to be sure, check the house before you leave. If Dam is laying in another room hurt, I want him found now." He hung up the phone.

Demetrius then met up with the other security guard. "I've got a situation. I need you standing guard directly outside of my wife's door. I'll square it with the doctor, but I don't want you to move while I'm gone. Got me?"

"I got it, boss."

Demetrius then took the kids in the room to see their mother. He told her. "I'm going to see if KeKe can watch the boys for a while. But I'll be back before my little girl comes into this world. Okay?"

"You don't think they want to stay? My parents are getting on a flight right now. They should be here in a few hours."

Demetrius shook his head. "They can see your parents later. You know how restless these boys get. They'll have the hospital torn down before the baby gets here."

"You might be right. I'll call KeKe, hopefully she's not at work today."

"If she is, tell her that I give her permission to take the day off. Tell her I'm on my way to her house and I need her to meet me there now."

"Don't be so bossy. I'll see what she says. Just have a seat while I make the call."

"I've got to go now, I want to get back before you have the baby. Just tell her what I said." He left her room before she could object further. Demetrius had to figure out what was going on before any of this found it's way back to his wife."

Todd called just as Demetrius was loading the boys into the car. "I checked every inch of the house. Dam isn't here."

Demetrius' blood was boiling but he tried to sound calm. "What about DeMarcus? What did the paramedics say?"

"He might need a blood transfusion, but he should be okay if he doesn't go into shock before they get to the hospital."

"Thanks Todd." Demetrius hung up and then called Al. He stepped away from the car so his sons couldn't hear him as he said, "I thought you were taking care of our problem?"

Al said, "I've almost got it handled. I'm sitting right outside his place, just waiting on some back up and then I'm going inside to get him."

"Are you sure he's there?"

"Most def. I watched him go inside with my own two eyes."

"I need you to go get that low-life now and hold him until I get there."

"You don't need to come over here. I've got this handled, " Al told him.

"That maggot just shot one of my sons and kidnapped my youngest son. So, forget about protecting me, Al. I'm in on this one. Alejandro is mine. This is personal and I'm going to end it."

DeMarcus had asked him to have his mother pray for them. Demetrius couldn't do that because he'd have to tell Angel that one son had been shot and another kidnapped. There was no way that he could put such stress on Angel while she was delivering their baby. So, he did the next best thing. When he dropped the boys off with KeKe, he sucked through his teeth as he apologized for the way he'd been treating her, then he asked her to pray as he quickly told her the situation.

Even though KeKe had become a Jesus freak, he trusted her and knew that she would never betray him.

~~~~

Maxine's head was laid against the headrest as she closed her eyes and relaxed. They were on their way to see about their daughter. Her last delivery had been terrible, so the moment Angel announced that she was pregnant again, Maxine made her promise to alert them the moment she went into labor.

She and Marvin wanted to be there for Angel, especially if Demetrius came out of the bag on her again. If Jesus didn't get a hold of that man soon, Maxine thought she might pop him one.

Marvin nudged her shoulder. "Maxine, wake up."

She opened her eyes, looked in her husband's direction and immediately saw the distress on his face. "What's wrong, I don't feel any turbulence."

"Something is wrong with Dam. I can feel it in my gut. We need to pray."

~~~~

Saul and a legion of warrior angels descended on earth with war on their minds. The enemy had stolen something that belongs to the Most High and they weren't leaving until they returned Dam to his rightful place.

"Do you hear that?" One of the warrior angels asked Saul. "The prayers of the righteous are going forth."

"Yes," Saul agreed, "But we will need many more prayers before the night is over."

"What are our orders?"

"Demetrius must rescue our charge. We cannot enter the building until Demetrius first finds the location. So, we must guide him here before harm comes to the child."

~~~~

"Give me my back pack," Dam demanded of his captors.

"I shouldn't give you nothing but a swift kick, the way you've been acting."

But one of the men stopped him. "Alejandro said we're not to touch the boy until he gets here."

"So, what are we here for? Are we babysitters or something?" one of them men sneered.

"For now, yes," The leader told them. "Now hand the boy his back pack and sit still for a little while. We are being paid handsomely to babysit this kid."

"Whatever." He went to the car and got Dam's back pack and then threw it in a corner.

Dam ran and picked up his back pack. He then sat in the corner and opened it. His race car was there, but so was his most favorite toy ever. His blocks. His grandmother had given the blocks to him and he had memorized the inscription on each block. As he took the first block out of his bag he said, "The Lord is my light and my salvation; whom shall I fear?"

He took the next block out, put it on top of the first and read, "The Lord is the strength of my life; of whom shall I be afraid?"

One of the kidnappers looked over at him. "What are you doing, kid?"

"I'm playing with my blocks." He took the next block out and said, "When the wicked came against me to eat up my flesh…"

Another block. "My enemies and foes, they stumbled and fell."

The last block. "Though an army may encamp against me, My heart shall not fear."

He then took his race car and drove it around and around his blocks until he knocked the blocks over. Once the blocks were down, Dam began building them again. And once again, as he put one block on top of the other he began his praise and declaration to God. "The Lord is my light…"

"Are you kidding me? Are we supposed to sit in here with this boy while he sings praises to God? I can't do it. I'm leaving." The man threw up his hand and left the building.

"What about you?" the leader asked the other guy. "Does this boy and his blocks scare you too?"

He shook his head. "I'm not leaving. But I'm going to shut this boy up once and for all." He lunged at Dam.

But the leader pulled him back. He put his gun to his head. "Now you listen to me. I'm not about to miss out on my money because you want to kill this kid."

"Then shut him up. I can't take all of this God and Lord stuff."

The leader walked over to Dam.

Dam looked at the man and said, "I'm not afraid."

"You should be," he told Dam as he snatched up his back pack and threw his race car, and condemning blocks into the bag. He then snatched Dam up by the arm, and drug him down the hall to the bedroom at the end of the hall. He threw him in there.

Dam bumped his head as he slid against the wall. He started crying.

"I thought you weren't afraid."

"You hurt my head." Dam rubbed his head as he glared at his kidnapper. "God's going to get you for that."

"And I'm going to get you... How does it feel to know you'll never see your parents again?" the man tormented Dam with his words, anxious for the moment when he'd be able to do more than talk. He slammed the door and locked it from the outside.

Nineteen

"Where is he?" Demetrius had murder in his eyes as he walked up to Al.

"I've got him tied up in the basement. He's thinking about whether he wants to die slowly or quickly, and all that depends on whether we get Dontae back safely."

"He doesn't have Dontae."

Al eyed him. "You told me that Alejandro kidnapped your youngest son. Did you not?"

"Yeah, but that's Dam, not Dontae."

The surprise shone on Al's face as he said, "So Angel finally told you, huh?"

"Told me what? What are you talking about? Forget it." Demetrius stepped passed Al. "We've got business to take care of downstairs. We can talk later."

Al, grabbed his arm and pulled him back. "If Dam is the one Alejandro's men has, then you need to know this now."

"Okay, what is it, Al?"

"He's your son."

"Demetrius held up a hand. "It don't even matter to me anymore. I know I was tripping at first, but I'm attached to Dam now. He's just as much mine as one of my other sons, and I would lay down my life right now to get him back."

"Yeah, I can see that. But I'm telling you that Dam is your son. I don't know why Angel hasn't told you yet, but Don did a kinship DNA test with the kid, and he's the grandfather, so that makes you the daddy."

Demetrius' eyes widened in shock. He knew nothing of any kinship test. If the test came back in his favor, why hadn't Angel said anything to him about it?" When did they take the test?"

"Don offered to do it last year, but Angel had to get an attorney and everything to get the process rolling, so he didn't actually take the test until about seven months ago."

"And I'm Dam's biological father?" the shock was wearing off a bit.

"You the man." Al poked at Demetrius' chest. "So, we're getting ready to take care of business for your son… you got me. This ain't no other man's child. And we are going to make them pay."

"Let's go." Demetrius was shaking as he stepped into the house to greet the man who had stolen his son. But it wasn't from fear or anger at that moment. Demetrius had ordered his wife to kill his own child and had treated both of them like they meant nothing to him when his orders weren't followed. It was his actions that had almost destroyed his family. Alejandro was just trying to finish the job. But Demetrius wasn't about to let that happen.

When he saw that Alejandro's arms were tied to a pipe that hung from the basement ceiling, he remembered seeing Frankie just like that with a knife in his chest. This was Al's and his father's favorite method of torture. They would tie up their victims and beat them with anything they could find, breaking bones, fingers and toes until the victim was at the point of begging to die.

Demetrius never had the stomach for this kind of thing. But if it meant getting his son back he would do what he had to. "Just tell me where my son is. All I want is my son."

Alejandro lifted his head. His face was black and blue from the beating he'd already taken. He opened his mouth and spit on Demetrius.

~~~~~

The enemy was thick in the air. Evil was descending on Saul and his troops. They unleashed their swords, ready for battle. "They're coming. This might be a long battle tonight. But we have to overtake them before they can get to Alejandro."

"We're ready," one of the angel's said as he swung his sword around, cutting down to demons as they tried to attack... and the battle was on.

"The child belongs to the Lord. You cannot have him," Saul warned.

But the enemy wasn't hearing that. He boldly proclaimed. "What makes him any different from so many other children of God that have come over to our side?"

"If they were truly God's children, then they will return and we will fight for them," the warrior angel said as he gutted the demon.

~~~~~

Demetrius wiped the spit from his face. Picked up one of the knives that Al had on his work table. He wanted to slit Alejandro's throat with that knife, but then he'd probably never find his son. So he plunged it into his thigh and twisted.

Alejandro screamed.

"Let me ask you again. Where is my son?"

"Why should I tell you?" Alejandro was panting from the pain but he kept on talking. "You stole my wife, Stole my life, and now you want your son back."

"I didn't steal your wife. I haven't had anything to do with Tricia in at least two years."

"Liar!" Alejandro spat.

Al picked up the iron that he had heated. "Pull his pants down," Al commanded. "I bet if I brand him, he'll start singing the tune we want."

Alejandro lowered his head and started weeping. He looked Demetrius in the eye as he spoke between sobs. "I never wanted anyone but Tricia... but you stole her away and made me kill her."

"Tricia is dead?"

Al said, "Move out the way, boy. I'll pull his pants down myself."

"No, Al. Wait a minute." For the first time in a long time, Demetrius felt the full weight of the guilt that belonged only to him. He had taken something from this man... something he had no right to take. And now Tricia was dead, Sammy was dead, DeMarcus was in the hospital with a gun shot wound that might end his football career and Dam was God knows where. The suffering had to end.

Al's method of pain on top of pain wasn't going to work on Alejandro. The man had killed the woman he loved, so he was living with the worst kind of pain everyday. Demetrius had to be real with this dude if he ever wanted to see Dam again. And Demetrius desperately desired to see his son again... he had a lot to atone for.

Truthfully, he told Alejandro. "You didn't have to kill her. I didn't want to be with Tricia. I love my wife and I'm sorry that I didn't respect the fact that you loved your wife too."

"You don't mean it. Just go ahead and kill me. I don't deserve to live without Tricia anyway."

"I don't deserve to live either, Alejandro. My actions destroyed both of our families. But my wife is real big on forgiveness. She forgave me for everything I did to her and to my son. So, now, even though I have no right to ask, I'm asking for your forgiveness, Alejandro.

"I stole something precious from you and for that I am truly sorry. But my wife has suffered just as you suffered. She didn't do anything to you. Her only crime is that of loving me and our sons. Please don't destroy her and my son for what I did."

"And if I tell you where your boy is, then what? Is Al going to stick that hot iron to me. And just keep torturing me until I die?"

Demetrius took the iron out of Al's hand. He unplugged it. "You have my word. I will not kill you. I just want my son."

~~~~~

Marvin and Maxine Barnes arrived at the hospital and went straight to the receptionist desk. "We're here for the Shepherd family?" Maxine told her.

The woman typed on her keyboard and then asked. "Angel or DeMarcus Shepherd?"

"DeMarcus? What is he doing in the hospital?" Marvin asked.

"Are you immediate family, sir?"

"I'm Angel's father and DeMarcus' grandfather."

"Well, let me write down the room numbers for you. I can't discuss your grandson with you, but you can go see him for yourself."

That didn't sound right so they headed to DeMarcus' room before going to see about Angel. Maxine was beside herself with

149

worry. "I feel so awful. We've been praying for Dam all the way here, and DeMarcus is the one in the hospital."

"Let's figure out what's going on before we start fretting over it," Pastor Barnes told his wife as they walked down the corridor in search of DeMarcus' room.

They found the room and entered. DeMarcus was laying in the bed, looking as if he'd been run over by a bus. "Oh honey, what happened?"

"Grandma! What are you doing here?"

"We came to be with your mom. But then we found out that you were in the hospital too."

Pastor Barnes asked, "Why are you here, DeMarcus? Does your mom know that you're in the hospital, because she didn't tell us anything?"

"I don't think Dad has told her yet. But I'm glad you're here. Can you both pray for Dam."

Marvin and Maxine looked at each other. Had they been right all along? Then why was DeMarcus in the hospital?

The nurse came into the room carrying a bag of blood. "Are you ready now?" she asked, looking a bit annoyed.

"No!" DeMarcus yelled at her. Then he turned to his grandparents. "She wants me to take that blood. But that blood could be full of Aids."

"That's just silly," the nurse said.

"Not too silly. I just read about someone contracting Aids from a blood transfusion." Pastor Barnes rolled up his sleeves as he told the nurse, "If my grandson needs blood, then take mine."

"We'll have to make sure that you're a match first, sir."

"Then get to matching," Pastor Barnes told her.

As Marvin left the room with the nurse. Maxine sat down next to DeMarcus and said, "Tell me what happened?"

"Some men broke into the house. They shot me and kidnapped Dam. You need to pray. Please pray, Grandma and tell Mama to pray too."

Maxine prayed with DeMarcus and then she went to the maternity ward to check on her daughter. She needed to know how Angel was doing, because if Marvin or she wasn't a match for DeMarcus, then Angel would have to be tested.

"Thank God!" Angel said as she watched her mother walk through her door. "I've been here all by myself for hours."

"Who is this man outside your door?"

"What man?" Angel asked.

"He says he's security."

Angel rolled her eyes. "Demetrius must have left that man at my door. I don't know what's going on, but he has a lot to answer for when he gets back here."

Now Maxine knew for sure that her daughter was clueless as to the things that had happened since she had been admitted into the hospital. She prayed that Marvin was a match for DeMarcus, because she didn't want to be the one to tell her daughter that DeMarcus had been shot and Dam was missing.

Twenty

Demetrius and Al drove to the spot that Alejandro said they would find Dam. They left him hanging in the basement just to make sure that he wasn't sending them off on some wild goose chase. Al left one of his men behind to watch over Alejandro.

Demetrius glanced at Al's artillery and got nervous. "How do you want to play this? We can't just go in blasting them, because we might hit Dam."

"Demetrius, I'm not going to put a bullet in your son. You might be new to this, but I'm true to this. Don't worry about me, I got this."

"Okay, I got you. But you brought that machine gun with you. And those things don't have eyes, they just keep shooting. So, I just want to make sure we watch out for Dam that's all."

Demetrius was scared out of his mind that he or Al might do something to cause one of the men inside the house to kill Dam. Even with a gun in his hand, he was so unsure of himself that he actually bowed his head and did what DeMarcus had asked... he prayed. He doubted that God would ever listen to anything a man like him had to say, but he was desperate and if Angel was right, Dam was born to serve God... so it was God's job to look out for Dam.

"You ready for this?" Al asked as he got out of the car.

Demetrius looked to heaven. "I sure hope so."

"He found the house," Saul said with glee in his voice. "Now all we have to do is get those imps off the front porch, the men inside will be easily dispensed once their evil protection is done away with. But remember, it is up to Demetrius to rescue the child. We have our orders. We cannot interfere with that."

"But if we can't help our young warrior, he might die during this battle."

"God help this earth if he does." The world killed Jesus and Peter and the Apostle Paul; and the angels were forced to stand by and watch as each had completed their Godly mission. But Dam's mission had not yet been fulfilled, so Saul prayed that Demetrius' love was strong enough so that he would fight with everything in him, to bring his son home safe.

The swords were back out. They would fight all night long if they had to. "Charge!" yelled one of the angels as he attacked the imps. The battle was going well for the angels, the only problem was, as one or two imps were slain, three or four more would take their place. Saul and his angels kept slicing and gutting each one that appeared.

~~~~

Al and Demetrius headed to the back of the house. The plan was to kick in the door and   blast the first person who ran towards them. But Demetrius didn't like that idea.

"Let me look through these windows first to see where Dam might be."

"Go head," Al told him. "I'll just sit here and play my imaginary piano."

Demetrius took his time, easing up to each window and poking his head up. Sweat dripped from his face with each step he took. It wasn't hot outside, but an inferno was boiling inside of him. Each window he looked in brought pain to his heart, because his son was nowhere in sight.

Demetrius whispered to Al, "These guys must be in the front of the house, because I don't see anything back here."

"I'll go look around front," Al said.

Demetrius pointed towards the side of the house. "I think there's another window around there. I'll go check that."

As the two parted company. Demetrius silently called on God again. "My son loves You. Please help us. Don't let these men kill my son." Demetrius didn't know anything about ending his prayers 'in Jesus Name'. All he knew was that he needed help, and he prayed that God would come see about Dam, even though his father was far from perfect.

He reached the window and slowly leaned his head over just enough so that he could see into the room. It was a small, dark room. At first glance it appeared empty, but Demetrius heard a sound, "The Lord is my light and my salvation, whom shall I fear."

And he instantly knew that Dam was playing with those blocks that he had wanted to throw in the trash. Thank God he hadn't. Demetrius lightly tapped on the window and whispered, "Dam, it's me."

Dam didn't respond so Demetrius tapped on the window again. "It's me Dam... it's daddy. Stand up so I can see you."

This time Dam responded. He said, "Daddy?" as he stood up.

Oh my God, it was Dam... his son was alive.

"Daddy, my head hurts," Dam told him.

Dam was just tall enough that he could reach the latch on the window. So, he told him to unlatch the window. But Dam either couldn't hear him or didn't understand what he needed him to do.

Demetrius said, "Stand back." Dam moved over as Demetrius lifted his foot and gave the window one swift kick. He had never kicked in a window before and didn't know if he would be able to get this one to open, but he was willing to try anything.

The entire window fell onto the floor. Demetrius didn't have time to marvel at what he had done, because he heard someone yelling from inside the house. "What's going on back there?"

"Come here, son. Grab hold of my arm so I can pull you out of there."

But Dam ran to his back pack and started putting his toys back in it. "We don't have time for that, Dam, we've got to go."

"I need my toys," Dam told him.

Then Demetrius heard the front door being kicked in and bullets flying. He didn't want his son in the crossfire, so he jumped into the room and grabbed his son and the back pack. One block was left on the floor.

Dam reached for it, but Demetrius said, "No, son. We've got to go." At that moment he could hear someone trying to unlock the door to the room Dam was in. He lifted his son out of the window and said, run.

Demetrius began climbing out of the window just as the door opened. The man lifted to gun to fire it, but was blasted with so many bullets that his body shook as he flopped onto the floor. Demetrius glanced over at the block that had been left on the floor, it said, 'my enemies and foes, they stumbled and fell'.

Al stepped over the dead man and looked at Demetrius. "You alright?"

"Yeah," he pointed to the block. "Can you get that and bring it to the car for me?"

~~~~

By the time Demetrius made it to the hospital with Dee, Dontae and Dam, DeMarcus had received a blood transfusion from his grandfather's blood and had been wheeled into the room with his mother.

Angel was bearing down, pushing their baby out. He ran to her side and held onto her hand. She shouted at him, "Where have you been? And where is my son?"

"Our son," Demetrius told her. "And he's right here."

Dam stepped into view and Angel let loose uncontrollable tears. She wanted to hold Dam, but she couldn't not just yet, because she had to push again.

"You can do it, Bae, just give it one good push," Demetrius coached.

"Don't you talk to me, Demetrius Shepherd. I'm so mad at you right now, I don't even want to hear your voice."

Demetrius glanced over at DeMarcus. DeMarcus shrugged. "I had to tell her, Dad. Papa had to give me blood and Mama started getting nosey about what was going on, so they wheeled me in here."

"It's not your fault son. I put this whole family in danger, but I'm going to make things right. I promise you all that."

"Don't give us empty promises, Demetrius. You've got a lot to make up for."

"Woman, will you stop yelling at me and deliver my daughter already."

And even though it had been a stressful situation for the entire family, the room erupted in laughter. And for the moment, that was enough.

Epilogue

Demetrius held his little girl in his arms and his eyes sparkled with love. His house was now complete. They had four boys and one beautiful little girl.

"What do you think we should name her?" Angel asked as she laid in her bed, trying to rest.

Smiling, Demetrius told her. "I'm going to leave that up to you, as long as the name begins with a D I don't care." Then he added, "Now, about Dam's first name…"

Angel shook her head. "Nothing doing. His name will not be changed. You'll just have to make do with the fact that his middle name begins with a D."

"Why didn't you tell me, Angel?" Demetrius wanted to know. "Why did you let me go all these months without knowing that Dam was truly my son?"

"I was planning to tell you. But in truth, I wanted to wait until I was sure that you loved me regardless. Because the way I see it, it's not just blood that makes us family… it's love."

"Alright Ms. Love-Makes-The-World-Go-Round. Can you tell me why Dam is so in love with that beat up race car and those blocks?" He still hadn't told Angel the full story of what Dam experienced and why everything went down the way it did. He didn't think that was a conversation for a woman who'd just given birth to the most beautiful little girl he'd ever seen. But he had to know why

Dam just couldn't leave that room without those toys when he had so many others at home.

"Well, my mother gave Dam those blocks when he lived with her. She helped him memorize those scriptures so that he wouldn't be afraid of things that he might face in life.

"And the race car was something that once belonged to you."

"I know, I gave it to Dee when he was little, but why does Dam like it so much? Why didn't you just buy him a new one?"

"Dam didn't care that it was old. He wanted it because it had been yours. Don't you get it, Demetrius? Your son loves you, even when he wasn't feeling much love from you."

Demetrius lowered his head as tears swelled around his eyes. Like Alejandro, he had allowed pride to take something precious from him. Alejandro had killed his wife, even though he still wanted her by his side. If Demetrius had gotten his way, his son would also be dead.

When he raised his head to face his wife again, he said, "You've taught me about forgiving others, even after they've done the most horrific things. But how do I forgive myself, Angel?"

Angel gently put a hand on her husband's neck. She leaned forward and kissed his forehead as she told him, "With man, that is a hard thing, but God can not only forgive your sins, he can cast them into the sea and remember them no more. When you're ready, I'll show you how to receive that kind of forgiveness."

Demetrius nodded. He didn't feel worthy of such a gift, but he was at least willing to consider it. "God must think something of me... He blessed me with this beautiful family and I can at least thank Him for that."

Looking towards heaven, Angel told Demetrius, "It is enough for now, husband. It is enough."

The end of Book III

Stay tuned for Book IV, The Children coming in February 2017

Don't forget to join my mailing list:
http://vanessamiller.com/events/join-mailing-list/
Join me on Facebook: https://www.facebook.com/groups/
77899021863/
Join me on Twitter: https://www.twitter.com/vanessamiller01